Eye of Itral

Author: Ken Spencer

Developer: Matt Finch

Editor: Jeff Harkness

5E Conversion: Edwin Nagy

Art Direction: Casey Christofferson

Layout and Graphic Design: Charles A. Wright

Cover Design: Suzy Moseby

Cover Art: Adrian Landeros

Interior Art: Brett Blakely, Thuan Pham, Sid Quade

Cartography: Robert Altbauer

Fantasy Grounds Conversion: Michael G. Potter

FROG GOD GAMES IS:

Bill Webb, Matthew J. Finch, Zach Glazar, Charles A. Wright, Edwin Nagy, Mike Badolato, John Barnhouse

Table of Contents

INTRODUCTION

The Eye of Itral is an adventure designed for 2–6 tier 2 characters. Characters skilled at finding clues, interviewing (or shaking down) informants, and operating within an urban environment will do best in this adventure, but a short trip outside the city and into the countryside of the Salchamp is called for and allows other types of characters their chance in the limelight. You can use existing characters for this adventure or create ones geared toward an urban investigation style; see **Appendix 2: Character Backgrounds** for options to make any class suitable for a noir-style investigation.

This adventure is an investigation set within the city of Cat's Cradle, as detailed in the *Cat's Cradle Sourcebook*. The centerpiece of the adventure is the *eye of Itral*, a magical artifact with a mysterious past desired by several powerful people. The characters become involved in the search for the eye, and with some skill and luck, come into possession of it. Owning the eye is no easy task, for the eye does not want to be owned, and since it is an artifact of great power and evil, the option to destroy it is certainly on the table.

The adventure is intended to be played in a noir style much like classic novels and films of that genre. No drawing-room detectives here, but the characters are cast into a hardboiled drama where they should not trust anyone, maybe not even each other. With the high stakes of high fantasy, there will be plots and plans, double-crosses, chases, and red herrings mixed in among the clues, as well as sharp, short fights. Murder is always an option, and some of the characters' foes certainly use such violence as a first option rather than a last resort.

RUNNING A NOIR FANTASY ADVENTURE

Noir is a genre of mystery or crime fiction that places a great emphasis on realism, duplicity, and ambiguity. While this does not seem well suited to a heroic fantasy game, it is largely a factor of adjusting your tone when running the game and encouraging your players to do the same. While you do not need to heed this advice when running *The Eye of Itral*, it certainly helps to bring the adventure to its fullest potential.

Realism does not mean an adherence to historical or scientific fact. The realism of the hardboiled detective tale is fairly far from the truth of the day-to-day life of a private investigator. Instead, it is an adherence to the motivations and actions of the supporting cast, of the NPCs. People behave as they would in a world where they exist as more than a list of clues they can provide. The people the characters meet have their own wants and needs: they pay bills, they have friends, they love (or hate in some cases) their families. They are not faceless mooks to be slain. The actions of the characters should have quick repercussions: shake down some shopkeepers, and the watch will show up; be too obvious about your investigation, and you will attract the attention of rivals and foes. Likewise, the setting should be gritty in its realism; the streets are a little dirtier, the alleys a little more shadowed, the taverns a little grimier. All should look lived in and not always well kept.

Trust no one, and keep your blade handy. It should always be expected that people are going to lie to advance their own agendas; the truth should not be easy to reach. Clues the characters find should never be straightforward; part of the fun of an investigation is piecing together the clues and sifting the lies from the truth. Three half-truths provide more fun at the table than one whole truth. This inherent duplicity should carry over into everything you describe to the players; even physical descriptions should be vague. For example, the mook is as tall as the door, or the box weighs as much as three sacks of flour or so. He went that way is better than he went north. Don't hold back information — just couch it all in a degree of uncertainty.

The villains of this tale, both the great and small, have their own motivations and are not in it for the evils. Some are motivated by money, others by power, and a few by religious fanaticism. They see nothing wrong with what they are doing. Indeed, despite their alignment, most see themselves as the heroes of the story. In other adventures, the characters might face dark lords and necromancers who are evil with a capital "E." The characters should feel some positive emotions about the villains of this adventure, or at least some empathy. The villains are not out to kill the characters; they have their own agendas that might make working with the characters the best option. Likewise, the characters' motivations for pursing the eye might not be noble, and the actions they take to get it might not be good. Characters in a noir-style adventure should be asking themselves if what they are doing is right or even if the goal is worth it.

ADVENTURE OVERVIEW

The Eye of Itral takes place in two phases, or "acts."

ACT ONE: PLOTS AND COUNTERPLOTS

The adventure opens with the characters coming to Cat's Cradle, either on their own or as advance agents for Fontaine or Heinrich. Early on, they run afoul of the Watchers of Itral and the fringe cult cell led by Nathar the Unwashed. Along the way, Tasker's Squad takes a dislike to them. The investigation into the location of the eye continues, and Stabvil is discovered as the best lead turns up dead. The rivals arrive in force, and a cloak-and-dagger drama plays out in the streets and alleyways of the city.

ACT TWO: THE SALT SKELETON

Once the location of the *eye of Itral* is revealed, it becomes a race to get it. (If the characters locate the eye and their rivals do not know, however, it won't be much of a race.) Naturally, the eye is not in any easy-to-find locale: It is deep within the fossilized remains of the Salt Skeleton. This act is much like a standard dungeon crawl, as it involves an expedition into the wilderness, a descent underground, and a quest for an item. Whoever comes out of the Salt Skeleton with the eye should be the winner, right?

INVOLVING THE CHARACTERS

You can involve the characters in the hunt for the eye in several ways. Which method you choose depends on what type of game you want to run. By default, it is assumed the characters are going to start off working for Elzara Fontaine or Jasper Heinrich. Both employ adventurers, though in very different ways. However, the characters might be an independent force in the hunt for the *eye of Itral*. Whichever hook you use, keep in mind that the characters should have their own agenda separate from their employer, if not at first, then by the second act. Only one person is walking away with the *eye of Itral*, and deadly means will be used to make sure of that.

AS A FOURTH PARTY

The characters might be a fourth party seeking the *eye of Itral*, at least at the start. During the adventure, they may ally with one of the other seekers and throw their lots in together, at least until the sudden and inevitable betrayal. For characters who are independent operatives:

• Academic, esoteric, or mystical characters may come across references to the *eye of Itral* and clues that it might be found in the Salchamp.

• You can place references to the eye throughout your campaign in order to build up to the reveal that it is in the Salchamp and might be tied to the Salt Skeleton.

• An anonymous patron might hire the characters to locate the eye. (Bonus points if that patron turns out to be Fontaine, Heinrich, or the Watchers of Itral.)

• Characters who are tied to a good-aligned religious order might be dispatched to locate the eye.

• Likewise, the same sort of organization might hire the characters to locate the eye, although paladins are notoriously bad at ferreting out information in the back alleys of cities (at least not without overly judicious smitings).

WORKING FOR ELZARA FONTAINE

Fontaine (see **Appendix 1: The Rivals** for more information on Fontaine and her crew) approaches the characters through an intermediary well before she plans to arrive in Cat's Cradle. The intermediary observes the characters from afar, taking note of their abilities and demeanor, and then openly approaches them to arrange a meeting with their employer. The characters are invited to a small estate outside of town whose owners are hosting Fontaine and her entourage (the host is thoroughly dominated by Fontaine and is kept hidden away in the attic until Fontaine leaves). Naturally the meeting occurs at night.

Servants in matching livery greet the characters at the door. Their cloaks are taken and neatly hung nearby, and they are allowed to keep their weapons and armor. All is elegance and taste, and the estate shows signs of having been redecorated. Fontaine waits in a modest sitting room down a short hall.

Elzara Fontaine's Offer

The well-dressed woman rises to greet you, proffering her hand in an elegant manner. She gracefully sits and gestures to the waiting servants who bring you trays of food and drinks, all in small measures so as to better accentuate their splendor. Once all of you have been served, she asks after your health, if you found the house with ease, and if you are planning on spending the night.

Once the niceties are taken care of, she gets down to business.

"I have heard of you, that you can be trusted, and that you are more than competent. Trusted is the greatest attribute in my mind; far too many people in this world are not worthy of my trust. Yet you, by reputation at least and appearance for certainty, are ones I can trust. I am but a widow, though with great wealth to support me. My interests are many, and my generosity and charity are unmatched in my homeland. I have come here because my agents determined that an artifact of great power, the *eye of Itral*, is out and about in the city. This thing, for it truly has no classification, is an artifact that cannot fall into the hands of dangerous parties. The Watchers of Itral, for example, are a dreadful cult that seeks to use the eye to awake the Salt Skeleton. How horrid.

I would request that you stop these fiends and any others seeking the eye for their own ends. As for me, I only wish to acquire it so that it can be studied and destroyed. I am not without means or arcane power myself, and I have many friends who can be relied upon for assistance.

I hope you will be numbered among them. I so greatly wish us to be friends, and if you cannot help me in this matter, at least enjoy a fine meal tonight, feel free to remain as my guests until morning, and be on your way with my blessings and wish for a fine tomorrow.

If the characters refuse the offer, they are treated to a feast that would be a gourmand's dream with a hostess well-versed in the social graces and quite knowledgeable about current affairs and arcane lore. If they choose to stay the night, there are comfortable beds, fresh linens, flowers in vases, and servants ready to meet any need.

Should the characters accept this offer, they will be well rewarded. Fontaine pays them 1,000 gp each up front to "cover her new friends' expenses," provides them a place at her estate, and allows them the use of her followers (save for Rivka) in their search for the eye. She also promises to make sure they are properly rewarded for their honesty and loyalty once the eye is recovered and destroyed.

"Thank you for proving the faith I have in you. All I know is that there are rumors that the eye has surfaced somewhere in the city. You should be careful in your search, for others want the eye for ignoble ends. I mentioned the Watchers of Itral. This cult will stop at nothing to fulfill its misguided prophecy. I know little else about them. There is another person, not nearly as openly fiendish or evil, named Jasper Heinrich. He wants to use the eye's powers to make himself a god. Being a vain, greedy, and rapacious man, I shudder to think what he would do with that power.

Support

Fontaine prefers to let her agents, in this case the characters, take the heat and do the dirty work. She will not become directly involved with them, but if they are captured or in a tight spot, she sends her vampire spawn to help them out, provided it is after sunset. Rivka is in charge during the day, and she is more proactive and helpful, though she is restrained by her mother's orders from direct action.

In addition to providing lodgings that are well guarded, Fontaine is willing to foot the bill for any reasonable requests. As time passes, she acquires contacts and dominated minions among the city's elite and uses these resources to aid her agents, but only if asked or if she feels it is necessary. She expects regular reports and to see some return on her investment, though she always couches her interactions in friendly terms and appeals to virtue.

Developments

While her charm and persuasive skills are where Fontaine starts, she wants to make sure her new agents are working in her best interests. She makes herself a close friend and understanding confidant for the characters and retains an appearance of a virtuous person slighted by her evil rivals. She plays as if good, if not lawful, and seeks to discourage violent plans but won't put up much of a fight if she sees a reward in their success, while at the same time placing any moral blame on the characters ("if that is what you think is best, but I find it distasteful").

The longer they are in her service, the more dangerous it becomes. If she manages to become friends with a character, she avoids dominating them. However, those who rebuff her offers of friendship are prime targets. Fontaine's favored strategy is to have one or two characters emotionally invested in their relationship with her, and one other dominated. That way, if any betrayal comes from the other characters, she has allies within the group.

Once the Eye is Found

Should a different faction locate the eye, Fontaine summons the characters to her and demands that they recover it at any cost. She relies on her friendships and other relationships, plays the part of an aggrieved party whose friends do not really care for her, and tries to use all her skill at manipulation to get the characters to act. If that does not work, she relies on magic and her ability to dominate in order to get what she wants. Those who fail her do not receive a reward, and their best hope to avoid becoming her next meal is to become completely dominated by her. If her minions are defeated and she has no more patsies to put into play, Fontaine retreats when her own personal might is no longer an assurance of victory. She is immortal and is willing to wait and rebuild her power before trying again.

If the characters give the eye to Fontaine, she rewards them as promised, with an additional 5,000 gp as a thank you for their help. Before they leave town, she, Rivka, and the vampire spawn attack the characters at night, preferably in a secluded place or in their lodgings. If possible, Fontaine attempts to keep them at her estate while setting up the attack. She does not like leaving any loose ends or witnesses.

Should the characters betray her, Fontaine's wrath knows no bounds. Despite the fact that she has been using and manipulating the characters, she sees their betrayal as a breaking of a friendship and seeks revenge through whatever methods she can. At first she chooses violence; after that, she uses more subtle methods to hunt them down and get back the eye. It is rightfully hers after all.

How She Intends to Use the Eye

Ever cautious, Fontaine spends the next few decades studying the eye. She uses it sparingly and then only to enhance her growing network of political power. In time she becomes the power behind the throne of a considerable empire: a dark, hidden queen whom the characters will recognize and might feel obligated to deal with.

Working for Jasper Heinrich

Heinrich (see **Appendix 1: The Rivals** for more information on Heinrich and his crew) meets the characters in a "cold call" situation, joining them in a tavern or visiting their lodgings with no preamble. He has only a bodyguard with him, and one whose orders are to remain as unobtrusive as possible. Always polite, Heinrich asks permission to join the characters or to enter their lodgings, handing his cloak and cane to his bodyguard before sitting down.

Jasper Heinrich's Offer

If the characters accept Heinrich's offer:

If they refuse Heinrich's offer:

The Calibos Inn is described in the *Cat's Cradle Sourcebook* (**Location G-2**).

Support

Heinrich has more money than he knows what to do with, and he also has access to a large collection of magical items. He willing parts with the former and begrudgingly with the latter if a case is made as to the need (only common and uncommon items, and he expects them to be returned). While he does not deploy many agents on the ground, his wealth allows him to bribe people far and wide. However, he prefers not to be directly involved and would rather give the characters the money for the bribe rather than send his personal agents to see to the task. Although he claims to find violence disturbing, Heinrich authorizes violence at the drop of a hat if it advances his agenda.

Working for Heinrich

Heinrich expects daily reports from his agents, at his lodgings if possible. If this does not happen, he sends Kavor or Misra to find out why. Neither is as polite as their employer and are rough, rude, and crass toward the characters. Injuring them attracts Heinrich's displeasure but not his wrath. Even his closest minions are merely tools to him. If the characters engage in illegal activity, Heinrich reprimands them for it only if they are caught.

Once the Eye is Found

Should a different faction gain the eye, Heinrich is furious. He spent good money and placed his trust in the character, and they failed. The only way back into his good graces and to avoid being his next target is to apologize and get the eye. At this point, Heinrich is willing to use all of his might and act openly in order to gain the eye. He enters the field of battle only as a last resort. Once the eye is in his hands, he has no use for failures and leaves the characters in the wind without any reward. Heinrich himself will not take the field, and if his minions are defeated, he retreats and tries again at a later date.

If the characters give the eye to Heinrich, he rewards them as promised with a 25,000 gp bonus provided they managed to get the eye without causing any official trouble to fall his way. He is genial and forgiving of any minor slights or failures, and exuberant in victory. When all is said and done, he leaves town the next day, promising to keep them in mind should he have further work for the characters.

Should they betray Heinrich and not give him the eye, he is violently wrathful and attacks at the first opportunity, even in broad daylight. There is no subtlety to his anger; he comes with his full entourage and attempts to take the eye by force. The death of the characters is of little concern to him; if they must fall in the pursuit of the eye, so be it. All that matters is the eye and that Jasper Heinrich possesses it.

How He Intends to Use the Eye

Heinrich begins the process of attuning to the eye and putting it to use as soon as he has it. This is to his misfortune, for he is soon lost in the eye, his mind subsumed by the desire to see and know, to possess knowledge of other things he wishes to add to his collection. Within a few weeks, he is nothing but an empty husk that stares into the eye until he passes out, only to awaken and resume. Within a month, the eye kills Jasper Heinrich and leaves a power vacuum that will not be easily filled.

Working for the Watchers of Itral

The Watchers (see **Appendix 1: The Rivals** for more information on the Watchers) do not present themselves as crazed cultists or mustache-twirling villains. Indeed, they seek out the characters, and Estavil Sukro approaches them in a public place to offer them a job. Naturally he is not dressed as a cultist and instead wears the modest garb of a merchant. He is friendly, perhaps overly so, and asks if he can join them for a drink and a chat.

The Watchers' Offer

If the characters accept Sukro's offer:

The Ragged Man's Warehouse is **Location O-22** in the *Cat's Cradle Sourcebook*.

Treesa's Pub is **Location O-18** in the *Cat's Cradle Sourcebook*.

If they decline Sukro's offer:

Sukro does not truly care if they take his money to stay away or not; he sends
6 **Cultist of Itral** (see **Appendix 3: New Creatures**) to attack them later.

SUPPORT

While having the eye nearby does limit the ability of the Watchers to
apply their divination magics, the sheer amount of divination magic at their
disposal allows them to sort through the readings and apply ritualized chants
and numerical transmutations to discern the accuracy of the information they
receive. While these techniques are largely useless with regard to the eye itself,
it does allow them to keep better track of their rivals. The main support the
Watchers provide is information, but it is information supplied in their unique
way. The characters regularly receive messages from the cult that lists the
probability of various events occurring, of rival's being in certain places, or of
certain actions being more or less favorable.

ONCE THE EYE IS FOUND

Should a rival find the eye, the Watchers call upon all of their might,
including the characters, to retrieve it. They use any means necessary once
their long sought-after prize is within sight. This includes violence, and with
the eye so close, their subtler talents are useless. As they are at a disadvantage
where it comes to violent actions, they need the characters' help to succeed.

If the characters find the eye and turn it over to the Watchers, they are
thanked and invited to join in the ritual to secure the eye from misuse.
Otherwise, the characters are free to go. The Watchers have what they want
and find the characters to be of little use at this point. The promised divinatory
aid will not be forthcoming.

If the characters betray the Watchers, the cult comes at them with all of
its power and attempts to violently gain the eye. Being fanatics, they stop at
nothing to get the eye and fight to the death for it. The Watchers show little
restraint and attack in broad daylight in a frontal assault.

WHAT THEY DO WITH THE EYE

The Watchers hope to use the eye to awaken the Salt Skelton. Once they
have the eye, they go to the Old City and perform the ritual at the "abandoned"
tenement (**Location O-20**). This requires the sacrifice of a dozen humanoids,
which have already been prepared. If the characters are accompanying the
Watchers to the ritual, well, a few more sacrifices shouldn't hurt things.
The ritual does not have the effect the Watchers desire, however, as the Salt
Skeleton does not awaken and the world is not altered. However, their souls
are sucked into the eye, which then teleports to a distant land.

THE HUNT FOR THE *EYE OF ITRAL*

Three parties are looking for the *eye of Itral* and may serve as allies or competition depending on how the characters approach finding the eye. All three are willing to serve as patrons, although they prefer to double-cross the characters once the eye is recovered. This assumes that the characters are not looking to double-cross an ally or patron themselves. In the hunt for a powerful artifact, all bets are off.

THE ROUTE OF THE EYE

There are three *eyes of Itral*. Two were stolen from the Salt Skeleton centuries ago, with much of the lore surrounding the eye based on reports of those missing orbs. Both of these eyes have been lost, the trails gone cold, and their whereabouts unknown to any party. That there are three eyes is also not known, even in circles that regularly hunt powerful artifacts. This is why reports of the eye being found are so shocking, and why multiple treasure hunters have been drawn to Cat's Cradle.

THE EYE DISCOVERED

Stabvil is just a small-time salt miner and not a very good one at that. Lacking a claim to any of the rich areas of the Salchamp, he chose to delve deep into the hills in order to find unclaimed deposits of high-value alchemical salts. He never made the big score, bringing up just enough to pay his meagre expenses and to keep his hope up. In his last exploration of the Salchamp, Stabvil managed to wiggle his way into the skull. The horrors he encountered there sent him reeling, and he fled as fast as he could, making his way through the sinuses by sheer luck and out the nasal cavity into the void beneath the skeleton's face. From there, he saw the eye and the eye saw him. He carried the eye away with him.

Stabvil found his way back to the spine and then up to the surface. In a daze, he wandered back to his hovel and laid low for a few days. He then hit the bars, telling his tale in exchange for the drinks he desperately craved. Long a source of humor for the more serious miners, no one took Stabvil's claims of having reached the skull, seen a great eye that looked at him, or any of his tale as true, and discounted them as just more of the old miner's ramblings and imaginings. However, other ears heard these things, and word spread.

One of those ears belonged to the Keljack siblings. These fraternal twins, Kesk and Kask, were just minor thieves and muggers who occasionally rode with some of the bandit gangs that plagued the Salchamp. While they did not believe in the Salt Skeleton legends, they did believe that old Stabvil had found something of value. They snuck into his shack one night and murdered him. They looted the place but turned up nothing other than a few coins and odds and ends that they sold to tinkers. To cover their tracks, they took Stabvil's corpse and tossed it into the sewers under the Rat Market. Kask found Stabvil's map that showed where the skull could be found, but being illiterate, she thought little of it. But she kept it anyway. The map was then sold to Hiras the tinker.

Before he died, Stabvil disposed of the eye. It creeped him out and disturbed his dreams. Plus, he found out that he had to keep staring at it every dawn and dusk or it would move. Not knowing where to stash it, he gave it to his daughter in a wooden box he sealed with wax and wrapped in old cloths. Baska was told not to open the box under any means and to keep it safe, as it was worth a fortune to the right person.

THE EYE ON THE RUN

The eye wants to return to its socket but has no means of doing that directly. Its random teleportation is unlikely to return it, at least not in thousands of years. It needed a mind that would not break under the eye's pressure but could be suborned to its agenda. It did not find one in Baska. The first time she found the eye outside of its box, she panicked and sought out her father, but she found his shack empty and disordered. Placing the eye back in its box, she heard its call and stared into it. The visions she saw filled her with knowledge she did not want or understand, but she knew how the eye functioned.

Armed with this knowledge, she sought out her sometimes lover Usra the Cunning, a small-time sorcerer and vendor of charms. Usra found her normal divination means unreliable, and they had been for some time. Matching up what Baska knew about her father's recent activities with the timing of the divinatory unreliability and eventual blackout, Usra deduced that the eye was the cause. She also deduced that the eye was valuable. The two quarreled, but

with Baska already suffering from the eye's paranoia-inducing powers and having stared into the eye more than once, she threatened to leave with the eye. Usra could not permit that and drove her friend and lover away with a fireplace poker. While she was doing that, the sun set and the eye left.

It would be two days later before the eye was found again. Pungent Pete, a street orphan, found the eye while digging in garbage in an alley off Rivergate Street. The eye quickly possessed him, but Pungent Pete was unable to maintain any sanity. By the next sun rise, the eye was loose again. In quick succession, it was picked up by Jrovan the carter, traded to Olia the tinker for a pound of tobacco and large chicken, lost in the warrens of the Old City again, and then found by the honey dippers Tal and Rast. The latter added it to their collection of oddities found during the course of their work.

THE EYE RETURNS TO THE SALCHAMP

Tal and Rast fell under the eye's spell, and the couple spent more time staring into it. They began to fight over the eye, and in the end came to blows. After three days, Tal ran off with the eye, and Rast pursued. Their loud argument was heard throughout the street called Ingrate's Walk. An individual named Greo, who often settled minor neighborhood disputes, intervened and took the eye away from the couple. At last the eye found a person able to withstand its effects and capable of being nudged toward taking it back to its socket in the Salt Skeleton.

Greo was a devout follower of the goddess Ceres and well known among the denizens of the Old City. He had a strong will and learned to stare into the eye rather quickly. Keeping it secure in his possession, he sought out aid in understanding it. He approached Neliara, a gray-robed priestess of Ceres, and learned a little about what it was, namely that it was a powerful and dangerous magical artifact and that it should be returned to where it was found. Thusly armed, he set out into the Salchamp to return the eye.

Not being used to the great outdoors, Greo quickly found himself in trouble. Out of water, lost, and exhausted, he lost control of the eye and it slipped away from him more than once. Recovering it took hours and added to his troubles. In the end, he made it back to the skull, but left a long trail of sightings of Greo and his strange package along the way.

Divested of the eye, Greo died in the caverns trying to get back. His donkey was more fortunate and wandered safely out to the Salchamp where the salt prospector Ystil found it. He recognized the brand on the donkey and returned it to Panhandle Stables (**Location P-5** in the *Cat's Cradle Sourcebook*), the stable that had rented it out.

A donkey might not seem like a good informant, but weeks spent with the eye on its back affected the animal. Peaches is a bit smarter than the average donkey and can recall the path it took to the cave of the skull, albeit not a direct route but the wandering trail that Greo had led it on. She can recount her path, though from a donkey's point of view, and would be willing to go along as far as the entrance to the cave. However, she needs to be rented or purchased. The experience has not altered her personality much; she is still a stubborn animal. However, once she realizes her knowledge is important, she expects to be treated accordingly. Oats are mandatory, but she also doesn't want to carry any packs (and hates being ridden), doesn't move at a great pace unless forced (and sits down on the trail if she feels she is being mistreated), and expects to lead a better life when the entire affair ends. A nice stable, her own stall, and no need to work would be a good start.

THE ACTION

Much of the action in this act takes place in the Old City District of Cat's Cradle. It should involve the characters trying to discover clues as to whereabouts of the eye and the various factions getting in each other's way trying to find the information and to stop each other from getting any information. This requires you to think strategically about the factions looking for the eye and to react to what the characters do. Use the guides in the faction's descriptions as well as the dirty deeds listed below to determine what happens, but much of this is dependent on the actions of the characters and their reactions to the various factions. You will have to stay on your feet and improvise, but hey, that's why you get to wear the big hat. Just keep in mind that the rivals are not omnipotent; there must be some justification for having them know something as simple as where the characters are at any given time. The factions looking for the eye — Elzara Fontaine, Jasper Heinrich, and the Watchers of Itral — are all aware of each other. They are also aware of the characters, especially if the characters are working for one of these factions and are not serving as a fourth rogue faction.

While the search for clues as to the whereabouts of the eye are the motivation for this act, the hunt for clues is not the only action going on. The various factions don't just want to be the first one to get the eye, they also want to make sure their rivals do not get it as well. Toward this end, they perform various dirty deeds, nasty tricks, and their own deceptions on each other in order to dissuade, waylay, confuse, and confound their foes. You should use these to draw out this portion of the adventure and to make it harder to get the right clues to locate the eye, but also to add more spice and excitement. But every faction is going to be invested in an investigation, giving some of them other issues to deal with, and encouraging them to commit their own dirty deeds and nasty tricks brings all the players into the action.

CLUES

An investigation runs off clues. Some of them false, some of them true. The following are lists of the types of clues characters can gather and stop their rivals from gathering. This list is not exhaustive, and it is better to give the characters some clues rather than leave them stumped with nothing to go on to drive the plot. These do not have to be true clues, just something to mull over so no one throws up their hands in frustration. Keep in mind that in investigative fiction, the author provides the clues to the protagonists (and the readers); it is part of your task to do the same.

RUMORS

Unless the characters received any specific information from their patron (in which case, refer to the section on Locations and Conversations for details), they are likely to begin the investigation by collecting rumors.

Rumors often contain partial truths, but they mutate in the telling. The story that made it to the ears of the treasure hunters is that one Stabvil of Cat's Cradle found the *eye of Itral*. Agents were dispatched, passages booked by the faction leaders, and the hunt began. This is where the characters come in, the hunt gets underway, and the noose tightens around the eye.

The following information, some of it blatantly untrue, can be found by asking around. This takes five hours for each attempt. During this time, characters must do one of the following: spend 15 gp buying drinks and paying off informants; succeed at a DC 15 Charisma (Deception, Intimidation, or Persuasion) check; or succeed at a DC 15 Intelligence (Investigation) check. All but the latter are active attempts to gain information; they can tip off rival agents (assume there is a 75% chance that a rival gains the same information as the character). An Investigation check implies sitting and listening to others, passively looking for clues, and otherwise appearing as just another person out and about. Success at any of these endeavors results in a roll on the table below. A character may get the same roll on subsequent attempts; nothing says every attempt to gather some information won't result in the same information being discovered more than once.

RUMORS IN CAT'S CRADLE

1d20	Rumor
1	Stabvil's just a crazy old failure, a salt prospector who never made it rich and never went entirely bust.
2	Someone is killing the beggars and outcasts in town. Some say there have been deaths down in the Old City.
3	Oh yeah, Stabvil, he had this weird bundle under his arm when he came up out of the Skeleton last time. Ran off into the woods with it.
4	Ain't no one seen Stabvil in some time. Best look up his daughter Baska over in the Old City.
5	The Salt Skeleton is a load of malarkey; it's just some rocks that the salts formed around. Nothing more than that.
6	I heard they found a corpse in the river drained of blood, some young guy fresh off the boats.
7	Lots of people asking questions. Weird questions about eyes and such.
8	Not many folks go up past Heartache Ridge.
9	The salts, they twist natural things up bad. You have to keep a look out for nasty creatures in the depths.

1d20	Rumor
10	If you are heading into the Salchamp, you'll need to get yourself a filter mask or you'll die of the salt lungs, like my Ma did.
11	There's a rich stranger staying at the Calibos Inn in the Gold District, throwing money around like water.
12	Some strange folks have been seen around an abandoned tenement southwest of the Haunted Lady. It's signposted as condemned, so they shouldn't be there. I'd say they were part of the thieves' guild, but they're strangers in town.
13	Hear tell there are lots of caves in the Salchamp. Some folks say that's where the stories of the Salt Skeleton come from, caves that look like bones on the inside.
14	Something happened to the beggar-boy Pungent Pete. He's been acting all weird of late.
15	Hiras the Tinker had this weird statue of an eye in his cart over on Grapnel Street. No, that was Olia the Tinker down by the docks. One of them. My cousin saw it, but he's headed back out into the Salchamp.
16	Tal and Rast, the honey dippers, had a big fight a few weeks ago over an eye. Those two never argue. Sweetest couple I've ever seen as long as you stay upwind of them.
17	I heard that damn fool Stabvil talking about Big Bat Cave. No one ever goes there.
18	Usra the Cunning has been acting strange, muttering about an eye and keeping to herself.
19	Old Man Greo took off for the Salchamp weeks ago, and no one's seen him since. His donkey came back though. Odd, Greo's not a salt prospector.
20	Ystil says he's seen some strange goings on in the Salchamp. He's in jail for drunken brawling right now. [**Note:** The town's jail is at location **C-10** in the *Cat's Cradle Sourcebook*, but that isn't actually where Ystil is to be found.]

LOCATIONS AND CONVERSATIONS

The following are scenes where the characters can investigate to gain some clues as to the whereabouts of the eye. Unless otherwise noted, all the locals they interact with are **commoners**.

1. INGRATE'S WALK

Asking around in the shops or with the street vendors of Ingrate's Walk easily gains information about the very public and very loud fight between Tal and Rast. The neighbors are a gossipy sort and spill the beans to anyone not obviously in a position of authority. They are also very religious and gladly talk to anyone who purports to worship Ceres or Sefagreth. However, any character who seems to represent the local officials is given the cold shoulder, and "No one saw nothin' at all." A successful DC 13 Charisma (Deception, Intimidate, or Persuade) will be needed.

The people spoken with reveal the following details (along with random gossip):

• Tal and Rast argued loudly for days over something they found while honey dipping, but the couple had been acting strange beforehand.

• Old Greo intervened, as he always does in the neighborhood, and took something from them to Neliara, a priestess of Ceres who preaches in the Old City.

• The next day Greo locked up his house and left for the Salchamp. That was weeks ago, and he hasn't come back.

2. GREO'S LODGINGS

Greo's lodgings are two small rooms on the second floor of a building overlooking Ingrate's Walk. The door is not locked, but plenty of neighbors are watching for strangers, even at night. A successful DC 15 Dexterity (Stealth) check is needed to slip in without raising a hue and cry. The inside is neat and tidy, with a bed in one room and a sitting area in the other. A few books are mostly religious texts of the goddess Ceres. A note pinned to the small table he eats at reads, "Gone off on a holy mission to the Salchamp. If I do not return, please tell my children I am dead and Neliara that I have failed."

3. Saltcrumb City
(Stabvil's Shack and Ystil's Hut)

The characters might visit Saltcrumb City to ask about Stabvil or Ystil.

The "city" is a cluster of huts against the outer side of the town's north wall, a transient community for miners staying near town, usually on a temporary basis, where they can purchase supplies or sell the results of their labor.

Note: Saltcrumb City is not located on the Old City map.

A. Stabvil's Shack: The particular shack where Stabvil stayed is small and unkempt. The door is slightly off the leather hinges and unlocked. Inside are clear signs of a struggle: blood splashed on the floor, overturned chairs, and scattered belongings of little value. The floorboards have been pried up. There is nothing of value.

Asking the neighbors what happened proves difficult. The people who live here have little and tend to be paranoid about strangers taking that from them. A successful DC 15 Charisma (Deception, Intimidate, or Persuade) check is needed. If successful, the neighbors reveal Stabvil was acting strangely. Several weeks ago, the Keljack siblings broke into Stabvil's shack and there was a fight. They left with his body for the Old City. The neighbors did not report this to the authorities as the Keljacks are known to kill witnesses and dump them (so it is said) in the sewers under the Rat Market.

B. Ystil's Hut: Asking about Ystil's whereabouts is much easier than tracking down information about the deceased Stabvil. Unless the characters seem to be associated with the town's law enforcement, the miners assume they are here to do business with the prospector and direct them to the hut where Ystil lives. Ystil is actually quite helpful provided the characters are forthcoming with a few gold pieces to encourage the conversation.

4. The Rat Market Sewers

The sewers under the Rat Market are described in **Location O-13** of the ***Cat's Cradle Sourcebook***. Once the characters identify an entrance grate (there are several), a successful DC 13 Strength (Athletics) check is needed to scale up or down, and the tunnel is only six feet wide at the base. Stabvil's corpse and a few others have ended up here in recent weeks. Anyone descending into the tunnel is attacked by 4 **salt mummies** (see **Appendix 3: New Creatures**), including the corpse of Stabvil.

5. The Panhandle Stables

The stables are described in **Location P-5** of the ***Cat's Cradle Sourcebook***.

Greo rented a donkey named Peaches at this livery. A salt prospector named Ystil brought Peaches back several days ago, without any sign of Greo. The livery workers gladly gossip about it: Ystil said he found the donkey out in the Salchamp near Big Bat Cave. They also tell anyone who doesn't look as if they are seeking to cause harm that Ystil can usually be found in Saltcrumb City. Peaches is at the livery, but she needs a few days to rest before being rented out again.

People

The characters might speak with the following people to gain some clues as to the whereabouts of the eye:

6. Tenement with Laundry (Baska)

This tenement is where Stabvil's daughter, Baska, lives.

This four-story building can be reached only by going through other buildings, which brings down the rent and makes it an ideal place for those who are particularly poor or down on their luck. The ground floor of the building contains a laundry (where Baska works), and the upper floors are rented out in partitions separated by boards with spaces between them.

Baska has not been having a good couple of weeks. Besides having a fight and breaking up with her lover Usra, she has been under the effects of the eye and is now certain her father is dead. She can be found at her home or at the laundry on the building's ground floor where she works. If approached, she is standoffish but a successful DC 13 Charisma (Deception, Intimidate, or Persuade) check yields the following:

> "Dad came to me weeks ago with this wild story about having found the skull of the Salt Skeleton, but everyone knows there is no such thing. He had this big stone eye with him and wanted me to keep it. He thought people were after him. Someone was, and they broke into his shack and killed him, I'm sure of it. There was blood everywhere, and his stuff is missing, even the locket with mom's silhouette. I took that eye and looked into it. Strange things were in it, so I went to Usra for help, but she stole the eye from me and threw me out."

7. HIRAS THE TINKER

Hiras the Tinker owns a small cart where he sells repaired goods, random objects, and fenced items on Grapnel Run. He doesn't like to talk about where he gets his things, but a successful DC 15 Charisma (Deception, Intimidate, or Persuade) check causes him to open up. He actually doesn't have much of a story to tell. He bought a map and locket off the Keljack siblings, but he doesn't know where the Keljacks are, other than that they are members of a gang that controls Scamper's Run. He also bought a stone eye from Jrovan the Carter. The eye disappeared the next day, just vanished, but Hiras will pay 10 gp to get it back.

8. JROVAN THE CARTER

Jrovan the Carter was last seen heading into the Salchamp with a load of supplies, but he should be back in a few days. He has little to say if tracked down on the road: He found a weird stone eye in the gutter on Rivergate Street and sold it to Hiras the Tinker for tobacco and a chicken. If the characters wait for him to return, they can track him down to the Carters' Guild (**Location 8**).

The Carters' Guild is a large building at the corner of Dancers Road and Rivergate Road. The carters are not a reputable organization and are prone to violence in support of their guild members. Most of the ground floor is devoted to storing carts, which are rented out to guild members. However, if the characters claim to be interested in renting the services of one of the carters, they are well-received and introduced to Jrovan when he comes in.

9. SCAMPER'S RUN (KELJACKS)

Kesk and Kask Keljack are running with a gang of toughs on Ingrate's Walk. If approached, the 2 **thugs** don't want to talk and just mock the characters. Any amount of force or intimidation brings in 8 more **thugs** who join in the fight to drive off the characters (but they scatter if half their number is slain or disabled). If caught or cornered, the twins reveal the following with a successful DC 15 Charisma (Deception, Intimidate, or Persuade check.

TESTIMONY OF THE KELJACK BROTHERS

> "Yeah, we hit that old salt coot's place. Got out with a few trinkets and a map. Sold it all to Hiras down on Grapnel Street. Dumped his corpse in the Rat Market Sewers, too. What's it to you?"

For more information about the gang situation in this area, refer to **Locations O-17** and **O-19** in the *Cat's Cradle Sourcebook*.

10. NOSEFLOWER STREET (PUNGENT PETE)

The urchin Pungent Pete (**commoner**, but unarmed) can be found on Noseflower Street. The boy is wild eyed and suffers from starvation, dehydration, and exposure. He scampers off if approached and shouts nonsense about how an eye is coming for him and everyone else. If caught and given some care, food, and drink, he opens up:

> "I found, found, found this eye of stone in one of the alleys off Rivergate Street. Can't remember which one. I looked into that eye, and it looked into me, and I saw things that I shouldn't 'ave and can't and don't and then I lost it. It just went poof while I slept and rolled away, and I don't wanna get it back ever again."

11. TAL AND RAST

The couple can usually be found at work throughout the city or at their home on Birdperch Alley. They do not want to talk about the eye, but a successful DC 15 Charisma (Deception, Intimidate, or Persuade) check gets them to open up. All they are willing to say is that they found the eye in the palace sump pit, kept it, fought over it, and gave it to Greo to get rid of.

12. USRA THE CUNNING

Usra the Cunning (**acolyte**) hasn't left her home since she took the eye from Baskra. She can be found on Tail's Twist by a sign touting her skills at fortunetelling and talisman crafting. Her door is unlocked and the inside of her one-room home shows signs of neglect, as does Usra. She is obviously sleep- and food-deprived and dehydrated, and she just rocks back and forth on her bed muttering about an eye. If comforted and fed, she reveals between her crazed mutterings that she lost the treasure of her life. Whether she means the eye or her lover Baskra is hard to tell.

13. TEMPLE OF CERES

The goddess Ceres is the Goddess of the Home and Midwives, Goddess of Healing, Mercy, and Patience. This three-story temple houses a chapel on the ground floor and contains the quarters of the priestesses on the upper floors. If anyone asks in the chapel to speak to Neliara, the priestess on duty summons her from upstairs.

Greo brought the eye to Neliara and consulted her on what to do. Neliara is unwilling to reveal the holy mission to outsiders but talks to fellow clergy of aligned or similar deities. Otherwise, she has to be talked into revealing what she knows with a successful DC 13 Charisma (Deception, Intimidate, or Persuade) check.

Speaking with Neliara reveals the following:

> "Greo, good hearted and always kind Greo, came to me some time ago with this stone eye that was causing trouble in his neighborhood. I did not know what it was exactly but I was able to determine it was an artifact of some power and great evil. It needed to be returned to where it came from so that it could cause no harm. Greo volunteered, and I took this as a sign from the goddess that he had been chosen for the task. Somehow I knew it belonged in Big Bat Cave somewhere in the Salchamp, so I directed Greo to go find the cave and return the stone eye to it. He left with my blessings weeks ago, but I have no idea what has befallen him. It is a mission from the goddess, so all must be right."

14. Abandoned Tenement

This is a three-story building that — on first inspection — appcars to be structurally unsound, and dangerously so. A rough wooden sign reads "Condemned by order of the baron. Do not enter." The building is actually in much better shape than it appears.

The tenement is described in further detail in **Location O-20** in the *Cat's Cradle Sourcebook*, but the additional detail is not relevant to this adventure.

The characters may investigate this location while following up on Rumor 12, in which case there is a good possibility they may learn of the Watchers' plans.

Dirty Deeds

The following events can occur at any time during this act or when the characters are in Cat's Cradle. Roll randomly each day or choose which one you want to happen. More than one event can happen per day if the hunt for clues is going quickly or if it begins to bog and a change of pace is needed. While some of these events present a combat, all of them are meant to harass, confuse, and ramp up the paranoia rather than to kill or seriously harm the characters. Many of these deeds involve members of the various factions. You can find more information about them in **Appendix 1: The Rivals**.

Ambush!

A street urchin (**commoner**) approaches the characters and claims to work for one of the factions pursuing the eye. This need not be a rival; it can easily be a patron or an ally. The child has been magically compelled to seek out the characters and deliver the message that they are to meet an agent (or the leader, depending on their relationships) of the faction that night in an alley off Noseflower Street in the Warrens. The child knows only that a hooded figure offered a coin and called the urchin over. After that, everything went fuzzy.

Waiting on the roofs above the alley are 6 **thugs**. They have been planning this all day and are wearing dark clothing. A successful DC 18 Wisdom (Perception) check is needed to spot them. Once the characters are in the alley, or if the thugs are spotted, each throws down a clay jar that bursts on the ground and releases a **swarm of alchemical grubs** (see **Appendix 3: New Creatures**). The thugs flee across the rooftops once they throw the jars. If any are captured, they give only a vague description of a hooded figure who hired them at one of the drinking houses in the Old City.

Arson

The characters' lodgings are set on fire. This is an extreme move, as fires are risky in densely packed cities made of wooden houses and lacking good fire control. The officials take this seriously — very seriously. Unless they have their own private home, the characters are likely staying in an inn, and it is doubtful they are guarding all parts of that inn at all times. The fire starts in the cellar or basement, and alchemical salts are used to make it grow faster. Poisonous smoke fills the building in moments (those breathing it must succeed at a DC 13 Constitution save or be poisoned until they spend an hour in clean air). The fire spreads rapidly and overtakes a room in every direction each round. Those who enter a room on fire or who start their turn there suffer 14 (4d6) fire damage. Several innocents need to be rescued. If the characters truly angered a faction — by harming the faction's leader, for example — agents are waiting outside to finish off anyone who escapes the inferno.

Assault

If the characters split up during their investigation, they risk being attacked by a rival faction. This attack occurs at night in a secluded location or possibly even at the character's lodging. Half of the attacking faction's manpower is dedicated to the attack. The first attack is meant to scare off the characters; the attackers retreat if the victim is incapacitated or if more than a third of their own number falls. If spotted by anyone but the victim, the attackers flee. The first attack should send the message that choosing to pursue the eye can be fatal. The next attack is more heartfelt and attempts to complete the promise of the first.

Alliance

An agent of one of the characters' rivals approaches them with an offer of an alliance. They all want the same thing, and there is no need to fight over it. Instead, they can combine their strengths and take out the other factions, clear the way, and then it is each for themselves. A tempting offer, if they can be trusted.

Bandits, Claim Jumpers, and Other Third Parties

Once outside of the city, all bets are off. While some authority exists in the Salchamp, there are also many places where ambushes, murders, and other dirty deeds can be committed. Plus, there is no shortage of people who are willing to do dire things for a small amount of cash. These thugs should be hired in a double blind; they do not know who they are working for or why, just that the pay is good and the target is supposed to be easy. Alternately, the hiring agent is disguised or claims to be working for a different rival; thus, any fallout is directed in a different direction. A **bandit captain** leads 2d6 + 10 **bandits** to attack the characters and will besiege a camp in order to create a longer delay than a simple assault would. They are not fanatics and retreat if the leader is slain or if half their number are dead. However, even if run off, grudges linger and they may later take advantage of an exhausted or lone target.

Bribery

Pass a note to each player and put something innocuous on it. Tell them not to share the information with each other. Go on to another event. After that event, pull each player aside and speak to them. Each faction makes an offer to a different character; if there are more characters than factions, then some people don't receive an offer. Pull them aside anyway. Discuss the history of the Roman Empire, share recipes for air fryer donuts, or just have a nice chat.

For those who receive an offer, refer to the opening bids in the **Introduction** for how to stage the scene and what is offered. The factions target the most likely character to be suborned; the Watchers won't try to bribe a paladin, for example.

Blackmail

A rival has information about a character, information that should not come out. This requires a character with a dark and sordid past, or at least a few misdeeds. If one does not exist, the rival manufactures the information in a believable manner. They then contact just that character and arrange a meeting in a public place. The rival's agent lays out what they know and what they expect in return. This can range (depending on how desperate that rival has become) from simply reporting on the character's plans (or their employer if working for one of the factions), to sabotage or even murder. The latter should target a different faction: For example, a character working for Fontaine might be blackmailed into sabotaging the efforts of Heinrich's agents. Of course, once the hooks are in, the control is so much easier to maintain and the price of silence escalates …

Doppelganger

A rival hires a **doppelganger** to impersonate Stabvil and run around town for a few days. The doppelganger makes itself obvious to the characters, but at a distance, and then leads them on a merry chase. It uses its shapeshifting powers to avoid pursuit; the characters get close to "Stabvil" and then he's not anywhere to be found. If captured, it surrenders and reveals its employer.

Fake Papers

A rival allows the characters to discover letters giving orders or sending information between their agents or, for a double blind, between a different rival's agents. This paperwork can be discovered in a variety of ways: on the body of a slain or captured agent, brought to them by a third party, or just lying in the road wrapped around three cigars. The papers should be a nice fat red herring, one so juicy that the characters go chasing off after it while their rivals go about their business.

False Clues

A rival discovers something that is false and makes sure that the characters find it as well, after taking steps to improve its apparent veracity. Alternately, the rival plants fake evidence. This can be something as simple as leaving a fake map of the Salchamp at Stabvil's shack that notes where the eye was found. Informants can be bribed to tell the characters a lie. False rumors can be sowed in areas the characters frequent.

False Friend

A rival's agent introduces themselves into the characters' trust. This should be someone minor, a stable hand who is eager to help, a tavernkeeper or server who makes small talk, or a street urchin always eager to run errands or keep a lookout. This person is a double agent and reports to their true employer on the characters' actions and plans and, if the moment is right, lets someone else in to perform a little sabotage or murder.

Frame Job

While murder seems like the go-to crime to use to frame a rival, it draws a lot more attention than something far simpler. The characters' lodgings are broken into and evidence of counterfeiting is placed. These false coins should pass a casual glance but be obvious to anyone who succeeds at a DC 13 Intelligence (Investigation) check. A small bag of coins placed in an out-of-the-way location helps to set the scene; the real work is mixing some counterfeits in with the characters' cash stores. After a few days of unknowingly circulating false coins, a visit from a local official (Sergeant Tasker, a **veteran**, would make a good choice and could be tipped off) should tie up the characters for a few days while everything is sorted out. A rival sitting in the dungeon is not one who is on the hunt.

The Mickey

Unless the characters eat and drink only what they make or procure and cook for themselves, they are going to have to purchase food and drink from somewhere. Randomly choose a character who has recently eaten or drunk from a public place. A character who fails a DC 13 Constitution saving throw is incapacitated for three hours, or poisoned for one hour if they succeed. If their companions do not take them to safety, the character is carried off by a rival faction, searched, stripped to their undergarments, and left in a random alleyway. The knockout poison could have been administered in a number of ways: a stranger could have slipped it into their food and drink, a cook or bartender could have been bribed, or a server could have dosed the food and drink. A few questions in the right places can uncover whoever is behind it and lead back to an agent of the faction responsible.

None-of-my-Business

In a clear case of none-of-my-business, the characters come upon a fight between two rival factions. They can intervene, sit and watch, or just move on as they care.

Official Harassment

One of their rivals tips off the local officials about the characters' nefarious nature. Sergeant Tasker's squad (a **veteran** and 4 **guards**) approaches the characters and demands to know what they are up to. He arrests them if they are doing anything illegal; if not, he questions them rather rudely, searches them, pushes them around, and then moves on. In the end, he lets them know that he is watching them and that he does not like their kind around here.

Pettiness

These dirty tricks are cheap and nasty things; use them at will and often to harass, humiliate, and delay the characters.

• Glue in the door locks, dipped onto stored valuables, or placed in sheaths of weapons left at a tavern's door check.

• Honey, applied in the night and left to get warmer and stickier in the morning, works as well as glue and attracts insects.

• Dead animals left in lodgings attract rats and give a clear warning. Especially fun if it is just a head.

• A jar of urine tossed through an open window leaves a nasty mess. Cat urine works best.

• Rent a room adjacent to the characters' lodgings and run a few agents out of it. These agents are blatantly obvious, they even greet the characters when they see them. The agents follow the characters openly, knock on the walls at night, ask them to speak louder, and otherwise become an obnoxious nuisance. At no point do these obvious agents engage in violence. If attacked, they call for the authorities.

Sabotage

This sort of dirty deed is best saved for use during the second act as the characters are searching the Salchamp for the eye. You can even start as they are preparing to leave, and sabotage can take many forms. Passive acts include buying up all of one type of equipment such as mining tools, donkeys, rations, or even filter masks (see **Appendix 4: New Items**). Another is to bribe a vendor to supply useless or damaged goods that masquerade as fine specimens. Once in the Salchamp, there is poisoning of water sources, changing trail markers, illusions to hide trails, rockslides, poisoning livestock, bribing locals to give bad directions, and even sneaking in at night and running off livestock. A lone person (or an agent disguised as a rival faction's follower) paid to follow the characters at a distance and remain visible but not actually harass the characters can cause all manner of delay and confusion.

Searched

One of the characters returns to his or her lodging to find that they have been broken into and tossed. Whoever did it lacked finesse or didn't care if the search was obvious. Maybe they just wanted to cause some damage. Whatever the motivation, furniture is broken, linens and bedding are shredded, and packs and bags are split open and the contents dumped. The job was thorough; any hidden items are found with the assumption that the searcher had a +9 on an Intelligence (Investigation) check.

Street Mob

As the characters move about the city on their various missions, they attract a growing number of beggars, day laborers, and street urchins (treat as **commoners**) who begin to follow them. At first it is two, and then three, and if they are not dispersed, the number swells to 10 + 2 per character. The crowd can be dispersed with a successful DC 13 Charisma (Intimidation, or Persuasion) check or paid off with a silver piece each. If not dispersed before the crowd reaches its maximum size, the large mob descends upon the characters, pushing and shoving, begging for food and coin, and otherwise drawing a great deal of attention while keeping the characters occupied for 10 minutes. Each character caught in the mob must succeed at a DC 13 Wisdom (Perception) check or later discover that a quick hand took something of value. Any violence levied against the wretches draws official attention, but first the common folk of the marketplace hurl insults and overripe produce at the characters until the would-be heroes leave the scene. All Charisma-based checks for the rest of the adventure that involve the common folk of the city are made with disadvantage as the news spreads of people with the perfidy to attack a mob of the blind, the crippled, and children. If any of the mob are caught and questioned, they describe a person matching the vague description of a minion of one of the rival factions who paid them a silver piece each to bother the characters.

Tail

One of the characters picks up a tail. This person can be spotted with a successful DC 15 Wisdom (Perception) check. If not spotted, the tail reports back to their faction with what the character did that day. The tail can be either someone who works for the faction or a cut-out (a person hired in secret by a faction to follow someone but has no other connection to that faction). If confronted, the tail tries to flee (treat as a **commoner** if a cut-out). Proper interrogation reveals who they work for or clues as to who hired them.

INTO THE SALCHAMP

The Salchamp is a hilly region north of Cat's Cradle and the source of much of that city's wealth. Here are found ripplestone and jade-marble, as well as the alchemical salts. The quarries are large productions that involve hundreds of workers and several large financial concerns. The stone is found in large masses that are easy to locate and pursue. The alchemical salts are not as concentrated and tend to be smaller deposits ranging from a few ounces to a dozen tons or so. By long tradition, smaller groups find and excavate the salts, though some of the larger financial powers of the city back these groups.

Hunting down salt deposits is a lot like prospecting for gold. A great deal of knowledge is needed to find a motherlode, but even then, hard work, perseverance, and luck play integral roles. By law, those seeking to establish a salt mine must file a claim with the baron, who in turn receives a percentage of the profits. In practice, many wildcat miners simply "forget" to file a claim, especially on a small mine or one that turns out to produce very little.

Lying far outside the city in the rugged hills, the Salchamp is a nearly lawless place. As it covers thousands of square miles of broken terrain, the baron's guards patrol only a few areas: those near well-used roads and the quarries or mines of large, wealthy concerns. The rest of the area is left to its own devices. This makes it easy for bandits and claim jumpers to operate, as well as wildcatters who seek to evade the baron's taxes.

TYPES OF SALT MINES

Not all salt mines are the same. Some in Cat's Cradle and elsewhere imagine salt miners squatting by a creek, collecting water in buckets, and then boiling it down to reveal the alchemical salts in all their myriad colors. While this is a cheap means of extracting the salt, it is not the most efficient. Most salt mines are dug out of the ground where large veins of rock salt are hauled out or where soils with dissolved salts are washed and then boiled. The bravest salt miners, and Stabvil was one such, delve into the many caves found in the Salchamp in search of easily accessed subterranean deposits. This last is by far the most profitable, but also the riskiest method.

BOIL

The common sight of a miner scooping out buckets of water and boiling it in large salt pans can be seen along the lower slopes of the hills. The large salt deposits are found in the hills, often buried under tons of rock and soil. Rainfall dissolves the salts and washes it downstream. Often, these salts precipitate out of the water onto stones, deadfall, or even along banks where the streams slow as they meander toward the lake. In these locations, salt miners scoop up buckets of water along the stream beds (and scrape off any precipitated salts), empty them into three- to four-foot-wide pans, and slowly boil away the water. Rich deposits need only a single boil, but those polluted with other dissolved solids might need to be rinsed and re-boiled several times to yield high-quality salts.

This method is the easiest and least dangerous. The best sites for these boil mines are lower on the slopes and thus closer to civilization and all the protection that affords. The heavy work is in moving water and gathering fuel for the fires. The former can be eased by creating sluices that divert the stream, though this risks angering those further downstream, while the latter is becoming increasingly more difficult as the lower slopes become denuded of trees. Most boil miners bring donkey loads of coal and firewood with them.

PLACER

The most common salt mines, especially on the upper slopes where the motherlodes of salt can be found, are placer mines. These are difficult to locate; one must know the area and know how to spot them, or time and effort is wasted. A miner usually begins with a small boil operation to determine the quantity and quality of salt dissolved in a stream. From there, it is a process of following the stream uphill to locate the source of the dissolved salts. Once a likely source is spotted, it must be dug up. This often requires deep pits or lengthy shafts tunneled into the ground. If the placer miner is lucky, the motherlode is rock salt that can be dug out and carried down. If not, the salts are mixed in with rock and soils and must be washed out, boiled, and sometimes boiled again to render alchemical salts that will fetch a nice price in Cat's Cradle.

CAVE

Cave miners are a special breed, and the other salt miners give them a wide berth. Many see them as crazed, and that estimation is often not far from the truth. Hundreds of caves, often large caverns and complexes of tunnels, are scattered around the Salchamp. Cave miners go into these caves to find raw deposits of rock salt. While the finds are rare, those who are lucky enough to survive the search and locate a rock salt lode can come down from the mountains rich beyond their wildest dreams. However, the caves are dangerous and tend to have a higher concertation of creatures altered by the alchemical salts. Furthermore, the caverns seem to affect a person's mind and body. Filter masks (see **Appendix 4: New Items**) are needed to avoid overexposure to the effects of raw alchemical salts, and something about the caverns warps the mind and creates delusions and paranoia.

DANGERS OF THE SALCHAMP

The Salchamp is not a safe place. The terrain is rugged, bandits are a threat, and the native animals are dangerous (the locals call the largest predator a tiger, but it is really a panther). Adding to this, the alchemical salts contaminate the air, soil, and water. This contamination can cause horrid mutations in otherwise nonthreatening life, and even animate the dead.

AIR

The air is hazardous around salt mines, especially in caves containing large alchemical salt deposits. For every hour spent inside an area subject to salt contamination, a character must succeed on a DC 8 Constitution saving throw (modified by their situation) or roll on the **Salt Contamination Effects Table**.

SALT CONTAMINATION DC MODIFIERS

Modifier	Factor
−1	Wearing a face covering of some kind
−1	In a ventilated area (outside or in a cave with artificial ventilation)
+1	Engaged in active exercise that hour (combat, climbing, running)
+1	Open wounds
+1	Drank contaminated water within the last 24 hours

SALT CONTAMINATION EFFECTS

d100	Effect
01–35	A personality trait, ideal, bond, or flaw changes for 24 hours.
36–45	Vivid hallucinations that play out your daydreams and cause you to be stunned for one minute.
46–50	One sense becomes occluded for 24 hours (disadvantage on all Wisdom [Perception] checks with that sense [roll 1d4]: 1=smell/taste; 2=touch; 3=hearing; 4=sight).
51–60	Alignment reversal for 24 hours.
61–65	Shakes. Whenever you roll a 1 on a d20, you drop everything in your hands.
66–70	Blinded for one hour.
71–80	Deafened for one hour
81–85	Intense cramping. Whenever you roll a 1 on a d20, you are stunned until the start of your next turn.
86–88	Suffer disadvantage on all rolls involving a single ability score (roll d6: 1=Strength; 2=Dexterity; 3=Constitution; 4=Intelligence; 5=Wisdom; 6=Charisma). This applies to ability checks, skill checks, saving throws, and attack rolls for one hour.
89–94	Gain a level of exhaustion.
95	Lose a hit die.
96	Suffer the effects of a *confusion* spell for 10 minutes.

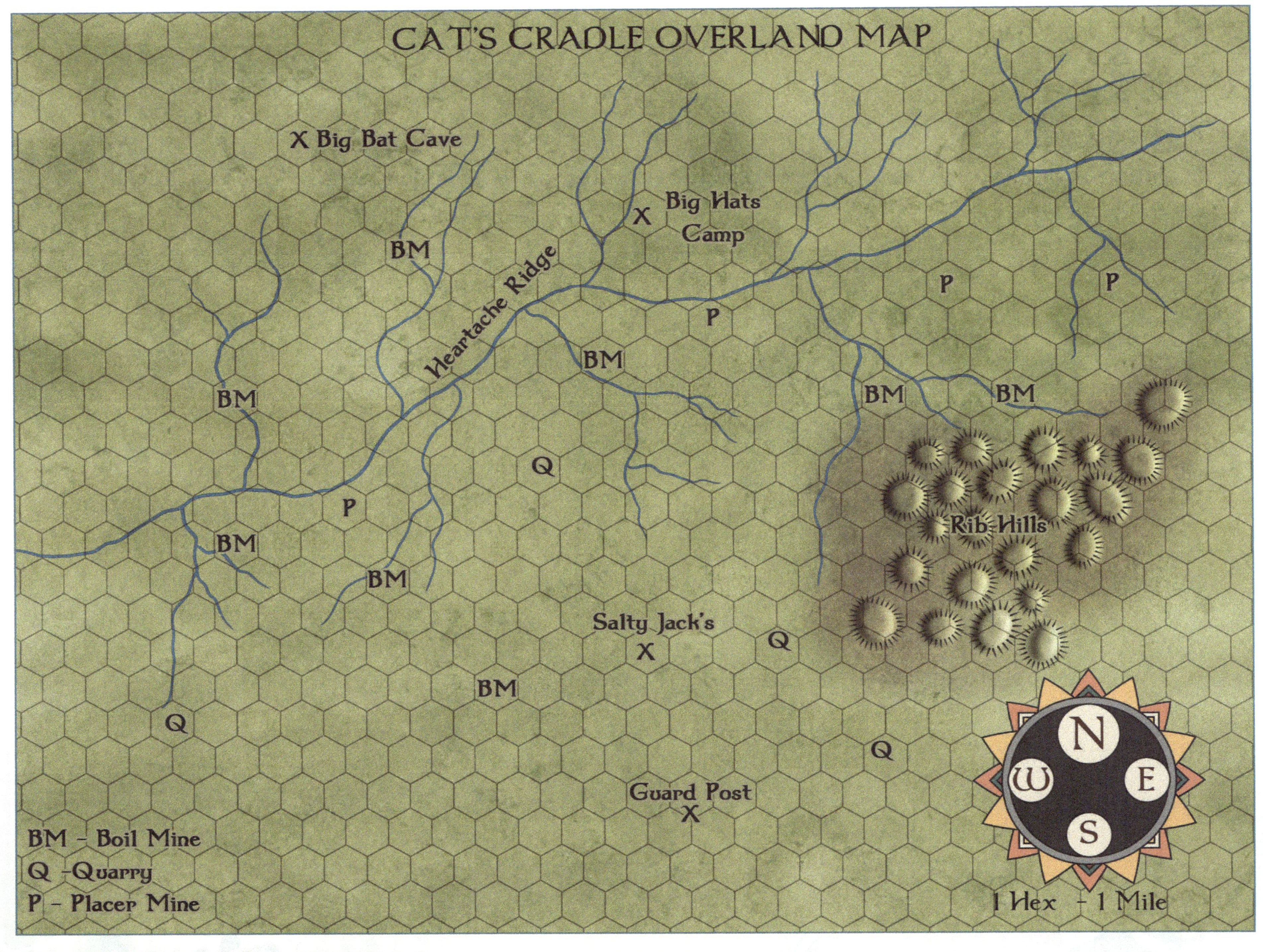

CAT'S CRADLE OVERLAND MAP
X Big Bat Cave
BM
Heartache Ridge
X Big Hats Camp
P
P
P
BM
BM
BM
BM
BM
BM
Q
P
P
BM
Rib Hills
Salty Jack's
X
Q
BM
Q
Guard Post
X
N
E
S
W
BM – Boil Mine
Q – Quarry
P – Placer Mine
1 Hex = 1 Mile

d100	Effect
97	Poisoned for one hour.
98	Frightened for one hour.
99	Petrified for one hour.
100	Roll on the mutations table (see the **Salt Mutant template** in **Appendix 3: New Creatures**). The effect lasts for one hour.

WATER

Much of the water in the Salchamp is not safe to drink as it is contaminated by the alchemical and natural salts. If boiled, it produces steam that can be collected and then drunk. With the right materials and a successful DC 13 Wisdom (Survival) check, a person could filter or boil the water to make it safer to drink. Both processes take at least an hour per gallon treated. The salt miners often keep a still going to produce fresh water for their own consumption, and some might be willing to sell or trade it at a rate of 1 gp per gallon.

WANDERING MONSTERS

The Salchamp is home to several unique monsters, with alchemical grubs, salt mutants, and salt worms (detailed in **Appendix 3: New Creatures**) being the most well-known, as well as natural animals, bandits, and other things. The alchemical salts have a variety of strange effects on living creatures and even corpses. Those who die in the Salchamp are usually cremated, but accident and murder often leave unburied corpses that are animated by the strange properties of the area. Check for random encounters every 12 hours; an encounter occurs on a 1–2 on 1d6, at a distance of 200 feet unless otherwise noted. This chance for encounter increases to 1–3 on 1d6 in the Upper Slopes, and 1–4 on 1d6 in the Deep Salchamp.

SALCHAMP TABLE

1d100	Encounter
01–25	2d6 miners (treat as **commoners** but armed with crossbows and axes, are indifferent toward the characters)
26–35	2d6 claim jumpers (treat as **bandits**, led by a **bandit captain**, attack only if they can do so from ambush, flee after losing half their number)
36–40	1d4 + 1 **swarms of alchemical grubs** (see **Appendix 3: New Creatures**)
41–50	Mountain tiger (treat as a **panther**, lost and confused, may be befriended, will flee)
51–55	1d4 **salt mummies** (see **Appendix 3: New Creatures**)
56–57	Minor earthquake (the ground rumbles, rocks slide down higher slopes, campfires have a 50% chance of getting out of control)
58–65	Salt wind (blows for 3d6 hours, everyone makes a Salt Contamination check, visibility is reduced to 50 feet for the durations, no rests may be taken without shelter)
66–75	Alchemical discharge preceded by a glowing and humming noise covers 20 + 5d10 foot radius centered on the characters and discharges within six seconds of starting. All characters must make a DC 13 Dexterity saving throw. Those who fail suffer 2d4 (roll d6: 1=acid; 2=cold; 3=fire; 4=lightning; 5=thunder; 6=necrotic) damage while those who succed suffer half damage
76–80	1d4 + 1 **salt worms** (see **Appendix 3: New Creatures**) spring from the ground and attack
81	Lost donkey (may be captured, is laden with 55 gp worth of common goods)
82–85	Abandoned miner camp (15 minutes of searching turns up 1d6 days of dried rations and one gallon of drinkable water)
86–90	1d3 salt mutants (choose a creature as the base and apply the template)
91	Miner's stash (a rock formation conceals 5,000 gp worth of pure alchemical salts in cloth bags, the miners [treat as **commoner**, but armed with crossbows and axes] are nearby and come to violently investigate; 50% the stash is trapped by a deadfall)
92	Exposed rock salt (a recently uncovered, modest-sized lode worth 1,500 gp but requires tools and 75 man-hours of work to uncover, weighs 55 pounds)
93–95	Rain (roll 1d6: 1–3=light rain for 1d6 hours; 4–5=steady rain for 1d4 days; 6=storm for 1d6 + 1 days)
96–98	Lone corpse of a miner, head bashed in, no valuables
99–100	1d4 crazed cave miners (treat as **berserkers**, attack in screaming fit, 50% chance of having a salt mutation, fight to the death)

SALCHAMP RUMORS

The investigation doesn't stop once the characters leave Cat's Cradle to search the Salchamp for the eye. Nor should the dirty deeds for that matter. The following information can be gained by asking prospectors, miners, and others encountered in the Salchamp.

SALCHAMP RUMORS TABLE

1d8	Rumor
1	The deeper you get in the Salchamp the stranger things you see. I was up past Heartache Ridge once, there were these … things … that gibbered and hopped, just masses of flesh.
2	Yeah, I once saw a bunch of lights in the Rib Hills. Tomuo followed them thinking they were lost miners. I stayed put, momma didn't raise no fools. Sure enough, Tomuo screamed, and the lights went out. I ran back upslope as fast as I could.
3	What you have to watch out for is shambling dead. No, hear me out, they dwell in the deeper hills and come out of the ground right at ya.
4	Ol' Stabvil was the one who went the deepest. Drove him mad. Blabbered on about ghosts of dragons and such, eyes that never blinked, and worse things. Nothing good happens past Heartache Ridge, I tell ya the truth on that one.
5	Some tenderfoot name of Greo came by, looked thirsty and lost. Gave him some water and pointed him on his way. Headin' for Heartache Ridge as I recall.
6	Seen a strange fellow pokin' around asking a lot of questions, just like you folks are doin', questions about eyes and such. Didn't take to him and told him nothin'. (This person can be described and is your choice of rivals.)
7	Yeah, heard of that Greo fellow, old man with no business out here. Asked about Big Bat Cave, or was it Tiger Cave?
8	Lots of strange folks about, bandits are all stirred up, and they say the tigers are howling in the deeper hills.

LOCATIONS IN THE SALCHAMP

The following locations can be found in the Salchamp. They should serve as locations for encounters and places to look for the eye. Keep in mind that there may be one or more factions moving on the map at this point in the adventure, and you should keep track of them. Spotting a rival or running into them in the dark should be fun. Feel free to add more locations to the map if needed.

Big Bat Cave

Located deep in the hills of the Salchamp, Big Bat Cave is far enough off the beaten paths and the locations where conventional wisdom says the best salt lodes can be found that few bother to go there. Desperate enough to try his hand at cave mining and foolish enough to ignore the advice of generations of salt miners, Stabvil headed off into Big Bat Cave. He found the eye there, lost his wits, and eventually this is the cave to which the eye returned.

Big Bat Cave is a natural cave carved by the action of thousands of years of water percolating through the soft stone of the Salchamp. The cave is at high risk of salt contamination. Increase the DC by +1 for **Locations BB-2** through **BB-4**, and by +2 for **Locations BB-5** through **BB-7**. No light sources are within the caves.

BB-1. Entrance

Sitting at the bottom of a steep hill, the entrance to Big Bat Cave is a 100-foot-tall and 30-foot-wide cleft in the hillside. The reek of bat guano fills the air for a dozen feet, and at sunrise and sunset **swarms of bats** pass through the cave's mouth. The tall cleft slopes down rapidly toward **Location BB-2**.

BB-2. Bat Cave

This wide and tall cavern (120 feet by 55 feet) is filled to a depth of six feet with bat guano (treat as difficult and frankly icky ground). A hundred **swarms of bats** are here, but mostly they do not move unless physically disturbed, and even then they are more prone to flying around at random than attacking. Any light source sets them to chittering and making noise that alerts the salt worms in **Location BB-5**.

The true threat in the bat cave is a colony of 10 **giant bats** that are salt mutants. These altered bats are vicious and cruel but tend to be sound sleepers. During the day, any loud noises disturb them and cause them to swoop to attack. The chittering of their smaller cousins is not enough to wake them.

BB-3. Hand Cave

The center of this 80-foot-diameter cave is filled with the fossilized remains of a great, six-fingered hand that thrusts up from the center of the room as if reaching for the ceiling. The fingers extend up from the floor to the second joint and then go on into the ceiling. The rest of the hand is buried in the rock above and below. Each finger is 10 feet across and made of stone much harder than that of the Salchamp hills.

Once every three hours, this hand regularly pulses with a greenish light. When it does, it deposits 1d4 **salt mummies** (see **Appendix 3: New Creatures**) that step out of the solid stone. At the same time, any salt mummies already in the cavern are absorbed.

BB-4. Salt Cavern

The two tunnels leading into **Location BB-4** narrow down to only two feet in width as they approach the cavern. The cavern itself is not made of stone; it is actually a 30-foot-wide by 300-foot-long fissure cut into a massive alchemical salt intrusion in the solid rock. The inclusion is a 500-foot-long, 50-foot-wide, and 200-foot-deep mass of high-quality salt. It is, unfortunately, not terribly stable, as it is incised with hundreds of cavities and voids of varying size. Anyone moving at more than half their speed through the cave runs the risk of falling into a cavity in the salt and must succeed at a DC 13 Dexterity saving throw or become mired up to their neck in the alchemical salts. This renders them prone and restrained (escape DC 15), but also requires an immediate Salt Contamination check.

A clear tunnel through the rock is beneath the salt in the southwest corner. It is only three feet in diameter and allows passage to **Location BB-6**. This cavity can be spotted with a successful DC 13 Wisdom (Perception) check. The secret tunnel is lined with salts and crawling through it triggers a Salt Contamination check. Any loud noises in this cavern attract the attention of the remains of Greo (**Location BB-7**). He is aware of the secret tunnel.

BB-5. Salt Worm Cave

Hungry salt worms tunneled out this cave to create a burrow here. It is small, 30 feet by 20 feet, and averages only eight feet in height. Lairing here are 3 **salt worms** (see **Appendix 3: New Creatures**) that attack any intruders but also investigate disturbances in **Location BB-2** or adjacent tunnels.

BB-6. Cross Passage

Three tunnels merge here, as does a hidden tunnel that leads to **Location BB-4**. This is the farthest spot from the skull (**Location BB-7**) where the thought ghosts can pursue. A hidden tunnel leads from here to below the salt in **Location BB-4**. This tunnel can be spotted with a successful DC 13 Wisdom (Perception) check, but it is only three feet in diameter and passing though it triggers a Salt Contamination check.

BB-7. Cavern of the Skull

The natural, water-carved tunnel abruptly stops at a formation that bears a close resemblance to a massive spine trapped within solid rock. The channel that would house a spinal cord is half filled with alchemical salts from which a narrow three-foot-wide by six-foot-tall passage has been scraped out. Following this 30-foot-long path leads to the massive hollow of the cavern, actually the open interior of the Salt Skeleton's brain case. The interior of the skull shows a network of indentations like a brain pressed into wet clay. Blue-white flashes of light travel along these, providing bright light inside the skull.

The skull of the Salt Skeleton rests facedown and forms most of this cavern. It is a massive formation with a great hollow cavity in the center. The mouth is filled with soil and is home to a nest of **alchemical grubs** that carved a network of tunnels that wind between the teeth and reach into the brain cavity. The skull has three large eye sockets, one of which houses the *eye of Itral*. In total, the skull is 600 feet from scalp to chin and 400 feet across at the temples.

Only one route through the open neck allows access to the skull.

Thought ghosts, memories, dreams, and imaginings of the Salt Skeleton lingered beyond its death and now form to defend the brain cavity and the *eye of Itral*. The thought ghosts are not true creatures, although the difference between a thought ghost and a snarling chimera might be slight to someone under its fangs. Thought ghosts use the statistics of a normal creature of their type, albeit one without much personality and dedicated only to protecting the eye and the brain cavity. They do have a few differences, however, as listed below:

* Thought ghosts are immune to poison damage.
* Thought ghosts are immune to the following conditions: charmed, exhaustion, frightened, petrified, and poisoned.
* Thought ghosts gain the following special features:

Ethereal Sight. The thought ghost can see 60 feet into the Ethereal Plane when it is on the Material Plane, and vice versa

Incorporeal Movement. The thought ghost can move through other creatures and objects as if they were difficult terrain. It takes 5 force damage if it ends its turn inside an object.

They also gain the following actions:

Etherealness. The thought ghost enters the Ethereal Plane from the Material Plan, or vice versa. It is invisible on the Material Plane while it is in the Border Ethereal, and vice versa, yet it can't affect or be affected by anything on the other plane.

BB-1
BIG BAT CAVE
BB-2
BB-3
BB-4
BB-5
BB-6
BB-7
BB-8
N
E
S
W
1 Square - 20 Feet

Ghost Body. As a reaction to being hit with a successful attack, the thought ghost can become insubstantial until the start of its next turn. While it is insubstantial, it gains immunity to acid, cold, fire, lightning, and thunder damage, as well as bludgeoning, piercing, and slashing damage from nonmagical attacks.

An infinite variety of thought ghosts can manifest. Choose a monster you feel would challenge the characters or roll on the following table:

THOUGHT GHOSTS

1d12	Ghost of …
1	3d8 **kobolds**
2	**chimera**
3	**wyvern**
4	4d4 **goblins**
5	**remorhaz**
6	**oni**
7	**minotaur**
8	**medusa**
9	**manticore**
10	**hydra**
11	2d6 **orcs**
12	**trolls**

BB-8. EYE SOCKETS

The slow process of soil formation covered the Salt Skeleton but left a large void beneath the face. This 20-foot-deep void is roughly 100 feet across and 300 feet along the midline and encompasses the three eye sockets as well as the nasal cavity and the upper jaw. It is pitch dark here, but small amounts of light leak in from the brain cavity through the two empty eye sockets and the nasal cavity. Although not enough light to see by, it does allow a delver to pinpoint those locations within the void. The eye sockets are aligned in a triangular pattern, with the one containing the *eye of Itral* sitting in the forehead above the two empty sockets. One minute after a living creature enters the void beneath the face of the Salt Skeleton, 1d6 **swarms of alchemical grubs** (see **Appendix 3: New Creatures**) tunnel up from the mouth and attack. They are by far the least fearsome guardians of the *eye of Itral*.

BIG HAT'S CAMP

Big Hat (**bandit captain**) is one of the more dangerous bandit leaders in the Salchamp. Striking from this hidden camp, he raids independent salt miners but stays clear of the larger mining camps and the quarries. He does this to avoid attracting much official notice. He is also smart enough to let most miners go after he divests them of their alchemical salts, the better to fleece them again another time. He sells the salts he collects to Hiras the Tinker in Cat's Cradle.

The camp is not much, just a few campfires and bedrolls in a box canyon. The gang consists of 20 **bandits**. Three stand lookout on the bluffs at the mouth of the canyon, while the rest can usually be found lounging around or performing various camp chores. The gang has 30 **riding horses** they keep at the back of the canyon behind a stick fence. There is a 25% chance the gang is out raiding at any time, in which case only the three lookouts and two keepers are at the camp. If not raiding, they have 1,500 gp worth of alchemical salts stored in the camp.

BOIL MINE

Two miners (**commoners**, but armed with crossbows and axes) work a small boil operation here. They are wary of strangers, but if approached kindly, they offer a seat by the fire, coffee, and beans. It is generally expected that visitors share some of their provisions as guests. The miners have been out here for a while and speaking with them yields a rumor or two.

HEARTACHE RIDGE

The commonly assumed marking line between the lower slopes and the deep Salchamp, Heartache Ridge gets its name from all of the prospectors who have crossed it and either never returned or came back emptyhanded. Worse, most come back with just enough wealth to outfit and head back, a tantalizing temptation of great riches that never materializes.

Quarry

Jade-marble or ripplestone are mined in large pit quarries that scar the Salchamp. The operations are extensive, with hundreds of workers toiling to cut out and haul up tons of rock. Well-supplied and well-organized, these quarries often have armed **guards**. They do not like strangers poking around and regularly run off prospectors and others who intrude. However, they are open to hiring new help. The work is exhausting, and labor is always in demand. Unskilled work brings in 5 gp a week plus food and water, while skilled stonemasons can expect 10 gp a week and better treatment.

Placer Mine

This larger mining operation is built near a suspected motherlode of alchemical salts. The ground around it is dug up, and a deep shaft runs into the hillside. The nearby creek was diverted to run through a sluice box, and all water downstream for 20 miles is polluted with alchemical salt runoff and is unfit to drink (adds an additional +1 to the DC of salt contamination). There are 10 miners (**commoners**, but armed with crossbows and axes) who are less than happy to see strangers poking around. They have accumulated 1d100 x 10 gp worth of alchemical salts and are leery of claim jumpers. If approached carefully, they willingly talk (and maybe share some rumors), but strangers are not welcome to stay, and any camp made within 10 miles draws their attention.

Rib Hills

These tall hills received their name from their shape. The sides of the hills are heavily eroded into long vertical gullies that bear a close resemblance to a rib cage of massive proportions. Those who support the Salt Skeleton hypothesis point to the formation as proof, while others just scoff at it. You can see anything in a cloud or a hill's shape. Even so, alchemical salts and jade-marble tend to be found here in larger concentrations than elsewhere.

Salchamp Guard Post

The only city guard presence in the Salchamp is a small fortified camp with a wooden stockade surrounding it. Inside is a well, a stout storehouse, and several tents for the 10 **guards** and their **veteran** commander. The guards are a font of knowledge as they spend most of their time watching travelers go past, speculating on said travelers, and gambling. They allow visitors to use the well and ride out if bandits are nearby or if a traveler is in distress within a few miles. Otherwise, they are content to sit and watch.

Salty Jack's

A stout, iron-banded wooden door is set into the rock face along the trail. A hand-painted sign on the door proclaims that it is the entrance to Salty Jack's. The door is locked (can be picked using thieves' tools and a successful DC 13 Dexterity check) and a lone **guard** remains on the inside. A small slot opens at head height if anyone knocks on the door, and a gruff voice asks who is there and inquires about their business. Those who answer politely are admitted to Salty Jack's, the only tavern in the Salchamp.

Nestled in a dry cave that has been expanded to accommodate the tavern, Salty Jack's walls are plastered over to keep the pervasive influence of the alchemical salts from affecting those inside. A deep shaft driven into buried aquifers provides fresh water.

The tavern is one large cavity dug out of the rock. The main room has a small fireplace with a flume that serves more to cook food than to provide heat or light. A six-foot-long wooden table is next to the fireplace, behind which are casks of ale and water, crates of foodstuffs, and a locked strongbox (can be picked using thieves' tool and a successful DC 15 Dexterity check) containing 75 gp, 50 sp, and 300 cp. Oil lanterns hang from hooks in the ceiling, but the lighting is always dim. Three tables, each capable of seating six people, are scattered around the room. A wider portion of the room to the south has eight three-tier bunk beds.

Three **guards** remain on duty at all times to keep the peace. Jackie Kilborne (half-orc **veteran**) owns the place and spends most of the day there. He retires to a nearby cabin to sleep or journeys into Cat's Cradle for supplies or to invest his proceeds.

Salty Jack's is a fine place to gather information about the Salt Skeleton. The regulars have experience mining the alchemical salts and are willing to tell tales both true and grossly exaggerated. Many of them work the deep Salchamp and have seen a thing or two. A few coins spent on drinks, some words among friends, and time spent socializing should yield a roll on the Salty Jack's Rumors Table. One hour grants a roll, or two rolls with a successful DC 13 Charisma (Persuasion) check.

Appendix 1: Rivals

The following three factions are vying for the *eye of Itral* and are willing to go to great lengths to get it.

Elzara Fontaine

Born to a simple peasant family, Elzara Fontaine was taken by a vampire shortly after her 23rd birthday. A slave to her vampiric master for more than a decade, Fontaine aided an adventuring party in slaying her captor and escaped with a portion of his treasury. She set herself up as a wealthy but eccentric merchant in various cities, moving on when suspicions began to gather. In this guise she has managed to stay just ahead of any hunting do-gooders and yet maintain a degree of wealth.

Along the way, she managed to grow her vampiric powers and supplement them with magical trinkets. While certainly far more mannered and skilled than the rude peasant girl she once was, Fontaine lacked a proper education in life. In undeath, she has learned to read and has studied arcane matters and history to a great degree but has not mastered more than the most basic of spells.

Through her networks of informants, she caught wind of the hunt for the *eye of Itral*. While Fontaine's knowledge of magical items is expansive, the *eye of Itral* is so obscure that she does not know much about it. Others want it and thus she has joined the hunt. Jasper Heinrich, her long-time rival, is involved, and Fontaine might desire his fall as much as she desires the eye.

As a person of wealth and power, Fontaine does not travel alone. She came to Cat's Cradle with a small entourage of 6 servants (**commoners**), 3 bodyguards (**guards**), and her personal attendant Rivka (who is Fontaine's daughter from shortly before Fontaine was kidnapped and turned, a fact that Fontaine keeps secret until the right time). Once in the city, Fontaine took no time establishing a local group of followers and now has 2 **vampire spawn** (Utiia and Zefon) at her beck and call, as well as 9 locals (**bandits**) whom she holds in thrall through her powers.

She has taken over a residence in the Jade District (the location isn't specified in this adventure, but if you do end up disclosing it, the Jade District fits best with Fontaine's personality) and uses it as her base of operations. She sleeps during the day in a coffin filled with grave dirt from her parent's grave mixed with the ashes of her former master. Naturally, she keeps that coffin well hidden in the cellar.

Elzara Fontaine

Elzara Fontaine is a **vampire** with the following additional feature:

Spellcasting. Fontaine is a 5th-level spellcaster. Her spellcasting ability is Charisma (spell save DC 17, +9 to hit with spell attacks). She has the following spells prepared:

Cantrips (at will): *mage hand, mending, prestidigitation, ray of frost*
1st level (4 slots): *comprehend languages, sleep*
2nd level (3 slots): *alter self, hold person*
3rd level (2 slots): *clairvoyance*

Rivka

A half-orc in her mid-30s, Rivka grew up an orphan given to the temples of the war god. She excelled at an early age, besting her fellow initiates in physical combat and at strategic games. In her youth, she had trouble controlling her battle rage. As she grew older, she learned to turn it into a seething source of cold fury. When Rivka reached maturity she left the temples, unwilling to dedicate herself to worship and leadership and wanting to see the wider world and maybe to find the parents who abandoned her. She managed the former, serving in several mercenary companies and earning her place as one of the finest warriors of her time.

Five years ago, she fell in with the wealthy merchant Lord Fontaine. While Rivka has no real recollection of why she chooses to follow this decadent and diffident woman, especially once she learned Fontaine was undead, she remains fiercely loyal. She serves as Fontaine's strong right arm, confidant, and often partner in planning the vampire's machinations. What Rivka does not know is that she is just a cog in Fontaine's machine. She is also unaware that she is the vampire's daughter, born months before her mother was kidnapped and cursed with undeath.

Rivka

Medium humanoid (human, orc), lawful evil

Armor Class 20 (adamantine plate mail, shield)
Hit Points 85 (10d8 + 40)
Speed 30 ft.

STR	DEX	CON	INT	WIS	CHA
20 (+5)	12 (+1)	18 (+4)	14 (+2)	10 (+0)	10 (+0)

Saving Throws Wisdom +3
Skills Intimidation +3
Senses darkvision 60 ft., passive Perception 10
Languages Common, Orcish
Challenge 5 (1,800 XP)

Loyal Bodyguard. If within five feet of Fontaine, Rivka may use her reaction when Fontaine is struck by an attack. The attack is applied against Rivka's Armor Class instead and, if successful, Rivka suffers the effects of the attack.

Relentless Endurance. If Rivka is reduced to 0 hit points but not killed outright, she can drop to 1 hit point instead. She can't use this feature again until she completes a long rest.

Savage Attacks. If Rivka scores a critical hit with a weapon attack, she can roll one of the weapon's damage dice one additional time and add it to the critical hit's extra damage.

Actions

Multiattack. Rivka makes two Longsword of Venom attacks.

Longsword of Venom. *Melee Weapon Attack:* +9 to hit, reach 5 ft., one target. *Hit:* 10 (1d8 + 6) slashing damage. As an action, Rivka can cause the longsword to become coated with a viscous black poison. This poison remains for one minute or until an attack using this weapon hits a creature. The creature must succeed on a DC 15 Constitution saving throw or suffer 7 (2d6) poison damage and be poisoned for one hour. The longword can't be used this way again until the next dawn.

Jasper Heinrich

A mage, regent of a powerful duchy, art collector, head of a small criminal enterprise, and dealer in illegal goods, **Jasper Heinrich** has come to Cat's Cradle for one thing, to find the *eye of Itral*. To achieve that, he will stop at nothing, but he would much prefer to get the eye using his normal means. Affable, charming, and sophisticated, Heinrich presents a different type of foe, one that the characters might willingly work with, and might willing work with them, for a time at least.

Born into a noble family, Heinrich received a first-class education. Never one to indulge in physical activities to any degree, he shied away from knighthood and mastered mystical arts to become an adept mage. Instead of appearing in ill-fitting armor on a horse he could barely mount, he offered his arcane services to his liege lord. This was deemed acceptable, and soon he had a position at court as his lord's personal wizard.

Heinrich used this position to enrich himself materially and politically. When his liege died and left a mewling babe as an heir, Heinrich maneuvered himself to become the regent. More wealth and power flowed his way, but the challenge was no longer great enough. He secretly dabbled in the black market and then defeated the local thieves' guild, taking over their operations under a new name. Much like his quest for legitimate power, this proved depressingly easy after a while. At that point, he turned to collecting rare art and magical artifacts, never minding if the current owner was alive, willing to sell, or any of that.

Catching wind of the *eye of Itral*, Heinrich has come to Cat's Cradle to personally oversee the hunt for the artifact. His small entourage consist of a bevy of servants (6 **commoners**), a troop of ducal guards (5 **guards** led by a **veteran**) and his personal aides **Kavor** and **Misra**. Using others such as the characters as go-betweens helps insulate Heinrich and his minions, but also provides convenient fodder if someone needs to take a fall or be thrown in the way of a rival.

JASPER HEINRICH

Medium humanoid (human), lawful evil

Armor Class 11
Hit Points 44 (8d8 + 8)
Speed 30 ft.

STR	DEX	CON	INT	WIS	CHA
8 (–1)	10 (+1)	12 (+1)	20 (+5)	16 (+3)	16 (+3)

Skills Arcana +8, Deception +6, History +8, Intimidation +6, Investigation +8, Perception +6, Persuasion +6, Stealth +4
Senses passive Perception 16
Languages Common, Elven, Draconic, Infernal, Primordial
Challenge 7 (2,900 XP)

Cloak of Displacement. Attack rolls against Heinrich suffer disadvantage. If he takes damage, the cloak is suppressed until the start of his next turn.
Spellcasting. Heinrich is a 7th-level spellcaster. His spellcasting ability is Intelligence (spell save DC 16, +8 to hit with spell attacks). He has the following spells prepared:
Cantrips (at will): *acid splash, light, prestidigitation, ray of frost*
1st level (4 slots): *charm person, detect magic, mage armor, magic missile*
2nd level (3 slots): *hold person, invisibility, suggestion*
3rd level (3 slots): *clairvoyance, dispel magic, lightning bolt*
4th level (1 slot): *arcane eye, dimension door*

Actions

Cane. *Melee Weapon Attack:* +2 to hit, reach 5 ft., one target. *Hit:* 1 (1d4 – 1) bludgeoning damage.

KAVOR

Heinrich's ablest henchman and the most loyal, Kavor is a young elf who worships his employer with almost religious fervor. The two are also lovers, though Heinrich often takes other lovers from time to time as his tastes vary. Kavor has studied much in his short 50 years and has mastered a few arcane arts as well as the sword and bow. Mostly he serves as Heinrich's chief bodyguard and most-trusted go-between. He has a haughty disdain for nearly everyone he meets and a chip on his shoulder about his youth so large that the *eye of Itral* could see it from its hiding place deep beneath the Salchamp.

KAVOR

Medium humanoid (elf), neutral evil

Armor Class 16 (studded leather)
Hit Points 82 (15d8 + 15)
Speed 30 ft.

STR	DEX	CON	INT	WIS	CHA
12 (+1)	18 (+4)	12 (+1)	14 (+2)	14 (+2)	14 (+2)

Skills Acrobatics +7, Intimidation +5, Perception +5, Stealth +7
Senses Darkvision 60 ft., passive Perception 15
Languages Common, Elven
Challenge 5 (1,800 XP)

Duelist. If fighting with a one-handed melee weapon, Kavor adds +2 to his armor class.
Fey Ancestry. Kavor has advantage against being charmed and magic cannot put him to sleep.
Loyal Bodyguard. If within five feet of Heinrich, Kavor may use his reaction when Heinrich is struck by an attack. The attack is applied against Kavor's armor class instead and, if successful, Kavor suffers the effects of the attack.
Spellcasting. Kavor is a 3rd-level spellcaster. His spellcasting ability is Intelligence (spell save DC 13, +5 to hit with spell attacks). He has the following spells prepared:
Cantrips (at will): *acid splash, mending, true strike*
1st level (4 slots): *burning hands, charm person, magic missile*
2nd level (2 slots): *flaming sphere, scorching ray*

Actions

Multiattack. Kavor makes two Rapier attacks or two Longbow attacks.
Flametongue Rapier. *Melee Weapon Attack:* +7 to hit, reach 5 ft., one target. *Hit:* 7 (1d6 + 4) piercing damage. As a bonus action, Kavor can cause his rapier to become engulfed in flames. These flames shed bright light out to 40 feet and dim light out to 40 feet beyond that. While ablaze, the sword deals an extra 7 (2d6) fire damage to any target it hits. The flames last until Kavor uses a bonus action to extinguish them, or until he drops or sheathes the sword.
Longbow. *Ranged Weapon Attack:* +7 to hit, range 150/600, one target. *Hit:* 8 (1d8 + 4) piercing damage.

MISRA

Slightly built, short, and with impeccable dress and manners, Misra is far too polite, calm, and serious to be Heinrich's favorite assassin. Yet the halfling is death in a three-foot sack. Bought from the slave pens in his desert home by the finest assassins' guild on the continent, trained to be a lethal machine, and then sent on his first mission, Misra refused to be a slave made to kill. Instead, he murdered his way out of the guild and his homeland to become a free man and assassin for hire. Along the way, he earned a reputation for his work and attracted the interest of Jasper Heinrich. Knowing that having one of the world's top assassins for hire in his employ improved his chances of completing the corrupt nobleman's various schemes and kept the assassin from being hired by a rival, Heinrich made Misra a generous offer, doubled it, and thus secured the foreigner's services. Misra is not truly loyal to Heinrich, but his agenda is to secure wealth, comfort, and freedom, things serving the corpulent mastermind provides. If the chance arrives to greatly improve his situation, such as getting the *eye of Itral* for himself, Misra takes a calculated risk.

MISRA

Small humanoid (halfling), chaotic evil

Armor Class 16 (studded leather)
Hit Points 67 (15d6 + 15)
Speed 25 ft.

STR	DEX	CON	INT	WIS	CHA
10 (+0)	18 (+4)	12 (+1)	12 (+1)	16 (+3)	12 (+1)

Skills Athletics +3, Acrobatics +7, Deception +4, Perception +6, Stealth +10
Senses darkvision 60 ft., passive Perception 16
Languages Common, Halfling
Challenge 5 (1,800 XP)

Boots of Elvenkind. Misra has advantage on Dexterity (Stealth) checks that rely on moving silently.
Murder. Misra is skilled at killing those who are unaware or distracted. If he has advantage on an attack roll, he inflicts an additional 14 (4d6) damage of the same type as the weapon used. He has advantage against any creature that hasn't taken a turn in this combat. In addition, any hit he scores against an opponent who is surprised is a critical hit.
Nimble Escape. Misra can take the Disengage or Hide action as a bonus action on each of his turns.
Uncanny Dodge. When an attacker that Misra can see hits him with an attack, he can use his reaction to halve the attack's damage against him.

Actions

Multiattack. Misra makes two Shortsword attacks or two Hand Crossbow attacks.

Hand Crossbow. Ranged Weapon Attack: +7 to hit, range 30/120 ft., one target. *Hit:* 7 (1d6 + 4) piercing damage and the target must make a DC 15 Constitution saving throw, taking 14 (4d6) poison damage on a failed save, or half as much damage on a successful one.

Shortsword. Melee Weapon Attack: +7 to hit, reach 5 ft., one target. *Hit:* 7 (1d6 + 4) piercing damage.

WATCHERS OF ITRAL

Sages, priests, and even the gods disagree on what the Salt Skeleton really is, where it came from, and how it ended up beneath the Salchamp. One theory is that it is the remains of the god Itral, a primordial divinity that died at the dawn of creation and was buried by the newly formed world. This is more than a theory for the Watchers of Itral; it is the foundation of their faith.

According to the Watchers, Itral willingly died so that their prophecy could come to fruition. The prophecy is interpreted to mean that the faithful will be rewarded when Itral awakens to rend the world in twain and usher in a new era of individual freedom and extreme license during which none may stop another from the fulfillment of their most primitive desires. Indeed, those primitive desires should be all that exists in this new world. The sky will fall, and with it the gods, and the faithful will at last be free to revel and rampage as they will, enjoying primal thrills that younger gods and mortal societies prevent. For the Watchers of Itral, the end goal is an era of psychopathy where the world burns and they dance around bloody altars.

A central tenet of this theological goal is to assemble the remains of their dead god in preparation to raising him from his death sleep. The continued mining of the Salt Skeleton is anathema to the Watchers and constitutes a gross waste of divine material in the pursuit of mundane power. Every day, part of their god is dug from its grave and carted off, and more runs off in streams and rivers. According to the Watchers, this is part of the plan of the younger gods and their dupes, the economic, political, and religious leaders of the world. Through this sacrilegious act, the enemies of the cult seek to prevent the return of Itral, at least according to the Watchers. In truth, few have heard of the cult, and the leadership of Cat's Cradle is unaware and unconcerned about it, at least at the beginning of the adventure.

Currently, the cult is working on a project they hope will speed up the rebirth of their dead deity. They hope to locate the *eye of Itral* that they believe was recently unearthed by the salt miner Stabvil. The cult will stop at nothing to get the eye but the members know they must not play their hand too openly lest they incur the wrath of the authorities. Once they have the eye, the cult plans to use it to contact the spirit of their deceased god through an elaborate ritual. Locating the eye is the primary goal of the cult's leadership.

POWERS OF THE FAITHFUL

Being a cultist of the Watchers of Itral is not just dressing up and attending some wild parties, or in the case for the street level beggars and ruffians who have formed cult cells, drinking to excess and brutalizing strangers. The theology of the cult is based around individual enlightenment through the meditations, transitive dances, and the use of various drugs and the alchemical drug thyst. This gives even the least initiated member of the cult a limited form of prescience, not enough to see the future but enough to sense when some momentous personal event is about to happen. Those deeper in the cult's methods gain greater powers.

CULTIST OF ITRAL

The rank-and-file of the Watchers of Itral are a mixed lot. Some are from the edges of society and want to bring it all down to lift themselves up, while others are jaded scions of wealth and power drawn to the cult to satiate their own desires. The cult is divided into small cells of three to nine members who tend to act independently but are overseen by high presentient. Even so, the cult is not well organized or ordered, and cells tend to pursue their own plans without guidance from the cult's leadership.

Most of the common cultists are armed with curved daggers that are the symbol of the cult. More "enlightened" cultists carry curved swords as a symbol of their advancement. (See **Appendix 4: New Items** for details on the cultic dagger and the cultic sword.) All wear leather armor under their robes, rags, and other clothes, for the cult encourages its followers to be prepared to defend their faith at any given moment. The esoteric disciplines of the common cultists grant them the ability to see threats shortly before they occur, resulting in desperate moves to avoid danger as well as an improved ability to detect coming danger. It is not foolproof, and magical effects tend to disrupt this prescience.

The leaders of cells are better armed and armored, wearing studded leather beneath their clothing and carrying curved swords. Their rituals reveal a variety of esoteric secrets, including some spells. They can also see much more of the future before it happens.

CULTIST OF ITRAL

Medium humanoid (any race), chaotic evil

Armor Class 12 (leather armor)
Hit Points 11 (2d8 + 2)
Speed 30 ft.

STR	DEX	CON	INT	WIS	CHA
12 (+1)	12 (+1)	12 (+1)	10 (+0)	12 (+1)	10 (+0)

Skills Deception +2, Insight +3, Stealth +3
Damage Resistances bludgeoning, piercing, and lashing attacks from nonmagical attacks
Senses passive Perception 11
Languages Common, Itralite
Challenge 1/4 (50 XP)

Limited Prescience. The cultist of Itral has advantage on saving throws against nonmagical effects. A cultist who takes damage from a magical source loses this ability as well as damage resistance until the start of their next turn.

Magic Weapons. The cultist's weapon attacks are magical.

Watchfulness. The cultist of Itral has advantage on Wisdom (Perception) checks.

Actions

Cult Dagger. Melee Weapon Attack: +4 to hit, reach 5 ft., one target. *Hit:* 4 (1d4 + 2) slashing damage. The cultist may use the dagger to cast *augury* once as a ritual. The cultist regains use of this ability following a one-hour ritual.

Cult Sword. Melee Weapon Attack: +4 to hit, reach 5 ft., one target. *Hit:* 5 (1d6 + 2) slashing damage.

CELL LEADER

Medium humanoid (any race), chaotic evil

Armor Class 13 (studded leather armor)
Hit Points 11 (2d8 + 2)
Speed 30 ft.

STR	DEX	CON	INT	WIS	CHA
12 (+1)	12 (+1)	12 (+1)	10 (+0)	14 (+2)	12 (+1)

Skills Arcana +2, Deception +3, Insight +4, Religion +2, Stealth +3
Damage Resistances bludgeoning, piercing, and lashing attacks from nonmagical attacks
Senses passive Perception 12
Languages Common, Itralite
Challenge 3 (700 XP)

Limited Prescience. The cell leader has advantage on saving throws against nonmagical effects. A cultist who takes damage from a magical source loses this ability as well as damage resistance until the start of their next turn.

Magic Weapons. The cell leader's weapon attacks are magical.

Spellcasting. The cell leader is a 5th-level spellcaster. Its spellcasting ability is Wisdom (spell save DC 12, +4 to hit with spell attacks). It has the following spells prepared:

Cantrips (at will): *guidance, resistance, sacred flame, thaumaturgy*
1st level (4 slots): *cure wounds, detect evil and good, detect poison and disease, inflict wounds*
2nd level (3 slots): *augury, locate object, spiritual weapon*
3rd level (2 slots): *clairvoyance, dispel magic*

Watchfulness. The cell leader has advantage on Wisdom (Perception) checks.

Cult Dagger. *Melee Weapon Attack:* +4 to hit, reach 5 ft., one
target. *Hit:* 4 (1d4 + 2) slashing damage.

Cult Sword. *Melee Weapon Attack:* +4 to hit, reach 5 ft., one
target. *Hit:* 5 (1d6 + 2) slashing damage. The cultist may use the
scimitar to cast *augury*, *clairvoyance*, and *legend lore* once each
as a ritual. It regains use of this ability following a one-hour
ritual.

Estavil Sukro, Watcher Presentient

The leader of the Watchers of Itral, or at least those in Cat's Cradle, is a
disaffected scion of a distant noble house. Born and raised in a life of ease and
sublime refinement, she chafed under the expectations of her position. Adding
to her dissatisfaction was that, as a younger child, she never had a role in the
family business. There were expectations that she would find a place in life in
a priesthood or, at the very least, as a patron of artists and a society leader. But
when her sorcerous powers began to manifest, Estavil turned toward arcane
studies, a forbidden topic in her family.

Delving deeper into her research, she learned of the many theories behind
the Salt Skelton, including the Watchers of Itral. At first intrigued by the
transgressive nature of the cult, she delved further, eventually making contact
with a cell composed of street beggars and others at the edge of society. The
thrill of the cult's rituals and the scandalous nature of associating with people
so far removed from her upbringing led her deeper into the cult.

Today, Estavil lives two lives. Most know her as a rich socialite who is the
patron of several artists, scholars, and a few groups of adventurers. To the
Watchers of Itral, she is the high presentient, the oldest and most powerful
member of the cult. Her mundane power is centered in her wealth and social
regard, which she uses to aid the cult and their plans. She keeps the cult in line
through magical might and extreme ruthlessness.

Estavil Sukro, Watcher Presentient

Medium humanoid (human), chaotic evil

Armor Class 15 (chain shirt)
Hit Points 143 (22d8 + 44)
Speed 30 ft.

STR	DEX	CON	INT	WIS	CHA
12 (+1)	14 (+2)	14 (+2)	16 (+3)	18 (+4)	16 (+3)

Skills Arcana +6, Deception +6, Insight +7, Religion +6, Stealth +5
Damage Resistances bludgeoning, piercing, and lashing attacks
from nonmagical attacks

Senses passive Perception 14
Languages Common, Itralite
Challenge 8 (3,900 XP)

Limited Prescience. Estavil Sukro has advantage on saving
throws against nonmagical effects. If Estavil takes damage from
a magical source, she loses this ability as well as her damage
resistance until the start of her next turn.

Magic Weapons. Estavil's weapon attacks are magical.

Spellcasting. Estavil is a 7th-level spellcaster. Her spellcasting
ability is Wisdom (spell save DC 15, +7 to hit with spell attacks).
She has the following spells prepared:

Cantrips (at will): *guidance*, *resistance*, *sacred flame*, *thaumaturgy*

1st level (4 slots): *cure wounds*, *detect evil and good*, *detect poison
and disease*, *inflict wounds*

2nd level (3 slots): *augury*, *locate object*, *spiritual weapon*

3rd level (3 slots): *bestow curse*, *clairvoyance*, *dispel magic*

4th level (1 slot): *divination*

Watchfulness. Estavil has advantage on Wisdom (Perception)
checks.

Actions

Multiattack. Estavil makes one Cult Sword attack and two Cult
Dagger attacks.

Cult Dagger. *Melee Weapon Attack:* +6 to hit, reach 5 ft., one
target. *Hit:* 5 (1d4 + 3) slashing damage.

Cult Sword. *Melee Weapon Attack:* +6 to hit, reach 5 ft., one
target. *Hit:* 6 (1d6 + 3) slashing damage. Estavil may use the
scimitar to cast *augury*, *clairvoyance*, and *legend lore* once each
as a ritual. She may do so once and regains use of this ability
following a one-hour ritual.

Saw It Coming (recharge 5–6). As a reaction, when hit with a
weapon attack or forced to make a saving throw, Estavil can
choose to have the attack miss or pass the saving throw.

Slippery. As a bonus action, Estavil can disengage and move up to
her speed.

Appendix 2: Backgrounds

The following backgrounds can be used for characters embarking on *The Eye of Itral* or in other adventures focused on investigation and mystery. While this adventure is designed for tier 2 characters, some players might be making new characters for this adventure, while others might lose a character during the adventure and want a replacement made to serve.

Former Cultist

Once you were a member of a cult, possibly even the Watchers of Itral. Something happened and you left. Perhaps you had a change of heart and saw that the cult's activities were foul. Maybe you were pushed out by political machinations within the cult. It could be that your friends or family took you from the cult and deprogrammed you. However it happened, you don't follow that path anymore, but fear you might be marked by it for life.

Skill Proficiencies: Arcana, Religion
Languages: The liturgical language of your former cult, most likely Abyssal or Infernal
Tools: Divination tools
Equipment: Former cult's vestments and symbol wrought in iron, sacrificial dagger, 10 gp

Friends on the Inside, Enemies on the Outs

You have a mixed relationship with your former cult. The hardliners want you punished for leaving, while those you were close to might be willing to help you out in small ways, possibly just to lure you back in. Likewise, you have reservations about using the knowledge you gained while a cultist; there are so many bad memories and regrets. Yet you know the insides of the cult better than anyone else and that knowledge might help bring them down, and even get those you care about out.

Jaded Socialite

Your world has been one of wealth and privilege — so much wealth and privilege that you struggle to find something that can move you. It is difficult to find a temporal delight that you have not explored, a delicacy you have not tried, or a privilege you have not leveraged for your own pleasure. You crave something new, anything new, to cure the ennui. Adventuring, involving yourself in death-defying activities, or chasing rumors of a new sensation are the only joys you have in this bleak life.

Skill Proficiencies: Deception, Performance
Languages: Any one of your choice, but the more exotic the better
Tools: Any one musical instrument of your choice
Equipment: Fine clothes, bottle of rare wine, various powders and substances of ill repute, 20 gp

Seen It All

Your pursuit of something to move your overtaxed senses and emotions has led you down strange avenues. Along those benighted routes, you have met all manner of people, mostly the type that people of your social class and breeding never encounter. To put it simply, you know people — and things that are not people — whom you have no right to know. They have provided a brief indulgence in the past, and might be able to provide information or a distraction from this life.

Knight in Sour Armor

You played the part of the hero once and swore to never do it again. Whatever it was you hoped to accomplish, you failed, and it cost you more than you could bear. But you did, you bore it and moved on. Now you stick your neck out for no one, at least until a cause comes along and you can't let things stand as they are. Time and again you are moved to act against your better judgment and get involved, and always to your detriment. You just can't let villains get away with their crimes or let the innocent suffer because you refuse to act. When you do, you grumble and complain, but you do what's right in the end.

Skill Proficiencies: History, Insight, Persuasion
Languages: Any one of your choice
Equipment: Common clothes, courtly clothes, memento from the last time you got involved, a simple or martial melee weapon you bring out only when called for, 10 gp

Ghosts of the Past

The previous times you placed everything on the line for a cause left more than just emotional scars; they have given you a web of contacts and friends. The people you helped remember you, at least those who survived, and would be willing to lend you minor aid. The last time you muddied your boots on the hero's journey took you to places you would rather forget, but those places might yield insight and clues to a new task.

Private Operator

You work for others solving their problems. While nobles and priests have their own people to handle affairs, your value is not just that you specialize in solving problems, but that you are discreet about it. Clients come to you with all manner of issues, most of them of the kind that they don't want publicly known. Dalliances that need covered up or revealed, thefts that the authorities either can't or won't solve, payments that must be made to people less discerning, these are the sorts of things you handle, and handle well.

Skill Proficiencies: Deception, Insight
Languages: Any one of your choice
Tools: Disguise kit
Equipment: Disguise kit, change of clothing, notebook in a secret cipher only you know detailing your cases, 15 gp

Informants

Your cases have led you into the halls of power and the lowest of slums. You know who to talk to in order to gain the information you need or the results your clients demand. Most of the time you communicate with these informants in disguise. Few know who you are, and most know only the beggar with the limp, the one-eyed sailor, or the foreign noble. Make sure you use the right disguise with each informant lest they discover who you truly are.

Vigilante

There are those who need to be punished but escape due to lazy authorities or by having the wealth and power to circumvent the law. Such matters will not stand, and you will not allow them to. Your normal persona cannot be involved or be seen to be involved, so you don a simple disguise and take the law into your own hands. Even those who aid you in this quest for justice might not know who you truly are, for if the truth gets out, those you care about, not to mention your standings in society, will be hurt. This is a risk you must take, for justice must be served.

Skill Proficiencies: Insight, Stealth
Languages: Any one of your choice
Tools: Thieves' tools
Equipment: Thieves' tools, dark cloak, scarf, 15 gp

Two Worlds

You move through two worlds, the seedy underbelly of the city and your daytime persona. This places you at risk of discovery, but also means that you have contacts and allies in both. Positioned as you are, you have access to knowledge and information, not to mention sometimes physical help, from both sources. You must be careful though, for there are dangers in the halls of power and the gutters, the greatest of which is that someone might discover that you bridge the two.

Appendix 3: New Creatures

Swarm of Alchemical Grubs

In my exploration of the so-called Salt Skeleton, I discovered that in the Salchamp it was not unusual for normal creatures to be affected, even mutated into new forms, by the mystical nature of the alchemical salt deposits. One of the deceptively dangerous mutations was the alchemical grubs. Deposited beneath the soil through means that many types of insects use to hide their young, these grubs feed upon the salt and are altered. Their flesh becomes spongy, almost airy, their bodies pale purple or green instead of the sickly yellow-white one would expect, their primitive minds linked into a gestalt consciousness greater than the sum of its parts. — Algrid Henswaith, University of the Vast

Scholars debate if the alchemical grubs are a new type of insect or the result of mutations affecting beetles and other insects. What is clear is that they do not exist outside the Salchamp, and even then almost always within the soil. Each grub is only an inch or two long and not terribly impressive physically or mentally. However, when they gather in larger numbers, they generate a telepathic bond that makes them dangerous. This allows them to better coordinate their activities and grants the swarm a level of intelligence and the ability to spontaneously generate magical effects.

Alchemical Grub Swarm

Medium swarm of Tiny aberrations, chaotic neutral

Armor Class 11
Hit Points 27 (6d8)
Speed 30 ft., burrow 20 ft.

STR	DEX	CON	INT	WIS	CHA
8 (−1)	12 (+1)	10 (+0)	12 (+1)	12 (+1)	8 (−1)

Saving Throws Constitution +2
Damage Vulnerabilities Fire
Damage Resistances bludgeoning, piercing, slashing damage
Condition Immunities charmed, frightened, grappled, paralyzed, petrified, prone, restrained, stunned
Senses darkvision 60 ft., passive Perception 13
Languages telepathy 60 ft.
Challenge 1 (100 XP)

Swarm. The grubs can occupy another creature's space and vice versa, and the grubs can move through any opening large enough for a Tiny creature. The grubs can't regain hit points or gain temporary hit points.

Innate Spellcasting. The grub's innate spellcasting ability is Intelligence (spell save DC 11). It can cast the following spells, requiring no material components.

At will: *levitate*
3/day: *magic missile*

Actions

Zaps. *Melee Weapon Attack:* +3 to hit, reach 0 ft., one target in the swarm's space. *Hit:* 11 (4d4 + 1) lightning damage.

Salt Mummy

[one possible place for alt mummy illustration]
The poor wretches used to be miners, people with families and loved ones, who expired in the depths of the Salchamp. They came shuffling at use, their mining tools raised to strike or dragging behind them. The three corpses were desiccated from the salts that still encrusted their undead forms. We put them out of their misery and moved on. Amateurs should not attempt the feats we do, even if driven by greed or necessity to enter a massive fossil. — Algrid Henswaith, University of the Vast

Salt mummies result when a person dies in the Salchamp and is left unburied. Most often, they are deep miners who ran out of water or food, were slain by monsters, or simply succumbed to the tainted air. More than a few are the result of murder, feuds, and claim wars that once ravaged the salt mines. Some theorize that salt mummies are also spontaneously generated by the weird stone formations scattered across the area.

Salt Mummy

Medium undead, chaotic evil

Armor Class 12 (natural)
Hit Points 60 (8d8 + 24)
Speed 30 ft.

STR	DEX	CON	INT	WIS	CHA
16 (+3)	8 (−1)	16 (+3)	8 (−1)	10 (+0)	2 (−4)

Damage Resistances acid
Damage Immunities fire, cold, lightning, poison
Condition Immunities charmed, exhaustion, poisoned
Senses truesight 30 ft., passive Perception 10
Languages none
Challenge 2 (450 XP)

Salt Explosion. If reduced to 0 hit points, the salt mummy explodes in a cloud of alchemical salts that fill a 10-foot cube. All creatures caught within this area must succeed at a DC 15 Constitution saving throw or suffer 3 (1d6) acid damage and must immediately make a Salt Contamination check (see table below).

Actions

Multiattack. The salt mummy makes two Fist attacks.

Fist. *Melee Weapon Attack:* +5 to hit, reach 5 ft., one target. *Hit:* 5 (1d4 + 3) bludgeoning damage.

Salt Breath (recharge 5–6). The salt mummy exhales a 15-foot cone of alchemical salts. Each creature in the area must make a DC 13 Dexterity saving throw, taking 21 (6d6) acid damage on a failure or half as much on a success.

"

Salt Contamination Check

For every hour spent inside an area subject to salt contamination (or for anyone caught within the salt explosion of a salt mummy), a character must succeed on a DC 8 Constitution saving throw (modified by their situation) or roll on the **Salt Contamination Effects Table**.

Salt Contamination DC Modifiers

Modifier	Factor
–1	Wearing a face covering of some kind
–1	In a ventilated area (outside or in a cave with artificial ventilation)
+1	Engaged in active exercise that hour (combat, climbing, running)
+1	Open wounds
+1	Drank contaminated water within the last 24 hours

Salt Contamination Effects

d100	Effect
01–35	A personality trait, ideal, bond, or flaw changes for 24 hours.
36–45	Vivid hallucinations that play out your daydreams and cause you to be stunned for one minute.
46–50	One sense becomes occluded for 24 hours (disadvantage on all Wisdom [Perception] checks with that sense (roll 1d4): 1=smell/taste; 2=touch; 3=hearing; 4=sight).
51–60	Alignment reversal for 24 hours.
61–65	Shakes. Whenever you roll a 1 on a d20, you drop everything in your hands.
66–70	Blinded for one hour.
71–80	Deafened for one hour
81–85	Intense cramping. Whenever you roll a 1 on a d20, you are stunned until the start of your next turn.
86–88	Suffer disadvantage on all rolls involving a single ability score (roll d6: 1=Strength; 2=Dexterity; 3=Constitution; 4=Intelligence; 5=Wisdom; 6=Charisma). This applies to ability checks, skill checks, saving throws, and attack rolls for one hour.
89–94	Gain a level of exhaustion.
95	Lose a hit die.
96	Suffer the effects of a *confusion* spell for 10 minutes.
97	Poisoned for one hour.
98	Frightened for one hour.
99	Petrified for one hour.
100	Roll on the mutations table (see the **Salt Mutant template** below). The effect lasts for one hour.

Salt Mutants (Template)

The bizarre environment of the Salt Skeleton can mutate natural creatures and breed strange beasts out of the remaining viscera. These creatures take a myriad number of forms, and no two beings are exactly alike. To create one, apply this template to a base creature, and alter its statistics and appearance as determined from the tables below.

Salt Mutant Template

A beast, dragon, fey, humanoid, giant, monstrosity, ooze, or plant can become a salt mutant. It retains all its statistics except as noted below.

Languages. The salt mutant cannot speak. If it could speak before its transformation, it gains telepathy 120 feet.

Mutations. The salt mutant rolls a number of times on the salt mutations table equal to it Challenge (minimum one roll).

Type. The creature is now an aberration.

Salt Mutations Table

1d20	Mutation	Effect
1	Tentacles	The mutant grows a 10-foot-long tentacle that it can use to make an attack that inflicts 3 (1d6) bludgeoning damage and the target is grappled. The creature can use Strength or Dexterity to make the attack and is proficient. The tentacle has an AC of 14, 15 hit points, and immunity to poison and psychic damage. Severing or destroying the tentacle deals no damage to the mutant, and severed tentacles regrow at a rate of one per day.
2	Extra Limb	The mutant has an extra limb (roll d6: 1–3, arm; 4–6 leg). If an arm, it may make one additional attack with that limb when it makes an attack action. If a leg, the mutant's speed increases by 10 feet.
3	Acid Excretion	The mutant excretes acid from its pores. Any attacks it makes with its natural weapons inflict an additional 3 (1d6) acid damage. Any creature that grapples the mutant or is grappled by the mutant suffers 3 (1d6) acid damage at the start of its turn as long as it is grappled.
4	Flailing Limbs	The mutant gains multiattack and may make up to two melee attacks as part of an attack action. If the mutant already has multiattack, it may make one additional melee attack as part of an attack action.
5	Camouflage Skin	The mutant has advantage on Dexterity (Stealth) checks.
6	Boils	If the mutant suffers piercing or slashing damage, the boils covering its skin erupt and all creatures within five feet must succeed on a DC 13 Dexterity saving throw or suffer 7 (2d6) acid damage from the putrid emissions.
7	Salt Breath	The mutant may use an action to breathe a 15-foot cone of alchemical salts. All creatures caught in this cone must make a DC 13 Dexterity saving throw, taking 18 (4d8) on a failure or half this damage with a successful save. The mutant can breathe a salt spray once, and regains use on a 5–6.
8	Elongated Limb	One limb that the mutant uses for an attack grows by 10 feet, increasing its reach.
9	Evil Eye	One of the mutant's eyes (or if it does not have an eye, it grows one) is warped and warty, but allows it to, as an action, innately cast *bestow curse* using its Wisdom as its spellcasting ability score.

1d20	Mutation	Effect
10	Extra Mouth	The mutant grows an extra mouth, and if it already has a head, an extra head as well. When it attacks, it can make an additional attack with the mouth as per its normal bite attack, or an attack that inflicts 3 (1d6) piercing damage if it does not already have a bite attack. The creature can use Strength or Dexterity to make the attack and is proficient. It gains multiattack, and if it already has multiattack, it adds a bite attack.
11	Eyestalks	The mutant grows a pair of long flexible eyestalks. As an action, it can make a ranged attack with these eyestalks, targeting up to two creatures within 60 feet. The ray from these eyestalks inflicts 7 (2d6) necrotic damage. The creature uses Dexterity to make the attack and is proficient.
12	Fast	The mutant's speed increases by 20 feet, and it gains advantage on Initiative checks.
13	Horns	The mutant grows a pair of horns that grant it a melee attack that inflicts 7 (2d6) piercing damage. The creature can use Strength or Dexterity to make the attack and is proficient. If the creature has multiattack, it adds this horn attack to its attacks.
14	Crazy Eyes	The mutant's eyes (it grows a pair if it normally does not have eyes) can be used to make a gaze attack. When a creature that can see the mutant's eyes starts its turn within 30 feet of the mutant, the mutant can force it to make a DC 14 Constitution saving throw if the mutant isn't incapacitated and can see the creature. On a failure, the creature is stunned for one minute. Unless surprised, a creature can avert its eyes to avoid the saving throw at the start of its turn. If the creature does so, it can't see the salt mutant until the start of its next turn, when it can avert its eyes again. If the creature looks at the salt mutant in the meantime, it must immediately attempt the save. While averting its eyes, any attacks on the mutant are done at disadvantage. A stunned creature may repeat the saving throw at the end of each of its turns, ending the effect on a success.
15	Armored Hide	The mutant's skin, hide, fur, or whatever is on the outside becomes hard and scaly, granting it a +2 bonus to its armor class.
16	Serpent Neck	The mutant's neck elongates by 10 feet, and if it does not already possess a bite attack, it gains one as Extra Mouth above.
17	Venom	The creature's bites and claw attacks carry a deadly venom. If the creature does not have a bite or claw attack, it gains the Extra Mouth mutation as above. The attack inflicts an additional 9 (2d8) poison damage and the target creature must succeed at a DC 13 Constitution saving throw or be poisoned for one hour.
18	Prehensile Tail	The mutant grows a 10-foot-long tail tipped with a sharp spike. When it makes an attack, it can make an additional melee attack with this tail (reach 10 ft.), inflicting 3 (1d6) piercing damage. The creature can use Strength or Dexterity to make the attack and is proficient. It gains multiattack, and if it already has multiattack, it adds the tail attack. Should the mutant have the venom mutation, this tail spike attack is also envenomed.

1d20	Mutation	Effect
19	Regeneration	At the start of the mutant's turn, as long as it has at least 1 hit point, it recovers 10 hit points.
20	Salt Tumor	The mutant has a massive tumor of alchemical salts within its body. When it dies, this tumor explodes, filling a 20-foot cube with alchemical salts and viscera. Any creature caught in this area must make a DC 15 Dexterity saving throw, taking 7 (2d6) acid damage and 7 (2d6) bludgeoning damage on a failure, or half this damage on a success. The creatures must immediately make a Constitution saving throw to avoid Salt Contamination. Creatures wearing filter masks do not automatically succeed on this saving throw, but do have advantage.

Salt Worm

It erupted out of the petrified bones that made up the walls of the tunnel. A great worm three feet in diameter and easily 10 feet long, its head sporting a pair of fanged mandibles that could shear straight through plate, muscle, and bone. The worm lunged out of the hole it dug through solid rock and took my bodyguard's arm. Straight through plate, muscle, and bone. I hit it with a simple incantation meant to freeze it, but it just shrugged off the blast of cold and came at me. — Algrid Henswaith, University of the Vast

Salt worms feed upon the alchemical salts found within the Salchamp, rats, and other vermin, as well as the occasional miner or explorer. They are multi-hued beasts with rubbery skin divided into numerous foot-long segments. Each segment has a pair of sharp-tipped claws that it uses to tunnel through solid rock or to dig through looser soil. These claws, as deadly as they can be, are not the creature's main means of attack. That primarily falls upon their sharp-toothed mandibles and acidic spittle.

Consuming alchemical salts in their unprocessed state is not recommended, and despite having some resistance to the salts, the worms still exhibit bizarre mutations. For some, this is merely cosmetic, their segments are all one color, covered in short hairs, or their mandibles are vertically placed as opposed to the more normal horizontal. Others have an excess of limbs per segment or can generate magical effects as part of their natural physiology.

Salt Worm

Large aberration, chaotic neutral

Armor Class 13 (natural)
Hit Points 90 (12d10 + 24)
Speed 40 ft., climb 30 ft., burrow 40 ft.

STR	DEX	CON	INT	WIS	CHA
18 (+4)	12 (+1)	15 (+2)	3 (−4)	12 (+1)	3 (−4)

Damage Immunities acid
Senses blindsight 60 ft, passive Perception 11
Languages none
Challenge 3 (700 XP)

Colors. The color of the head segment determines some of the salt worm's damage immunities and vulnerabilities, as well as the type of damage its alchemical discharge causes:

SALT WORM HUE

1d6	Hue	Immunity and Damage Type	Vulnerability
1	Blue	Lightning	Force
2	Red	Fire	Cold
3	Purple	Radiant	Necrotic
4	Green	Necrotic	Radiant

1d6	Hue	Immunity and Damage Type	Vulnerability
5	Orange	Force	Lightning
6	Silver	Cold	Fire

Mutations. The salt worm rolls on the Salt Mutation Table as per salt mutants.

Spider Climb. The salt worm can climb difficult surfaces, including upside down on ceilings, without needing to make an ability check.

Actions

Multiattack. The salt worm makes one Bite attack and two Claw attacks.

Bite. *Melee Weapon Attack:* +6 to hit, reach 5 ft., one target. *Hit:* 13 (2d8 + 4) piercing damage.

Claw. *Melee Weapon Attack:* +6 to hit, reach 5 ft., one target. *Hit:* 7 (1d6 + 4) slashing damage and target is grappled (escape DC 14). The salt worm can grapple only one target at a time and has advantage on Bite attacks made against a target it has grappled.

Alchemical Discharge **(recharge 4-6).** The salt worm discharges a 15-foot line of energy from its mouth. All creatures caught in this area must succeed on a DC 14 Dexterity saving throw or suffer 17 (5d6) damage of a type determined by the color of the salt worm's head.

Appendix 4: New Items

Eye of Itral

Wondrous Item, artifact (requires attunement)

The *eye of Itral* — and there are three of them floating around out there — is a powerful artifact with strange and disturbing powers. Many legends have sprung up over the centuries — and have been largely forgotten — concerning the eye's powers and dangers. To possess the eye is said to lead to untold mystical powers, temporal wealth, and even the chance to become a god.

Once removed from its socket, the eye starts to wander. At each sunrise and sunset, the eye teleports itself 1d10 x 10 feet in a random direction. It never buries itself or teleports into the air, and instead moves in a roughly lateral direction along the surface of the world, or if inside a cavern, remains on the floor. It can teleport and imbed itself in an inanimate object that is less dense than granite, displacing the matter of the object. However, when it does this, it always leaves part of itself, no more than one-third of its circumference, outside the object. The only way to prevent this teleportation from occurring is to have someone focus their vision in the eye's pupil during the hour-long period of sunrise and sunset.

While the eye is loose, divination magic is greatly affected. Any divination magic used or targeting a creature, object, or location with 10 miles of the eye returns a false result 50% of the time and gives no clue that the result is false. Within five miles, this false return rate increases to 75%. Within one mile, divination magic simply does not work, and the spell or power is expended but no answer is given. The eye itself is immune to this effect and its divination magic is unaffected. These false readings vary by the nature of the divination magic. Some simple magics that give yes or no answers give the wrong answer. Others that show an area, provide directions to the location of a target, or otherwise give more expansive information simply show the wrong location, direct to the wrong target or give false directions, or otherwise provide erroneous information. There is a 5% chance each time divination magic is used that instead of the normal effects of the magic, the result is a roll on the **Eye Effects Table**.

Staring into the eye is a risky affair. It is an artifact not of this world, alive in a sense but cold stone in another. Interacting with it poses dangers to the body and soul. Anyone who stares into the eye for even a moment receives visions of other worlds and of this reality, though rarely in a coherent form. Before staring into the eye, characters must declare how long they intend to do so, either for a few seconds, a minute, an hour, or multiple hours. During this time, the character is incapacitated and can only stare into the eye until the duration ends. While the powers of the eye are granted only to the character attuned to it, anyone can spend time staring into the eye.

At the end of this period, you must attempt a Wisdom saving throw with a DC dependent on how long you stared into the eye. The base DC is 15 and increases by +2 for each timeframe longer than a few seconds (+2 for a minute, +4 for an hour, and +2 for each hour after the first). If you fail, add +1 to the roll on the **Eye Effects Table**, with an additional +1 for each timeframe longer than a few seconds (an additional +1 for a minute, +2 for an hour, and +2 for each additional hour). At the end of the time you spend staring into the eye, roll on the **Eye Effects Table**.

Eye Disruption and the Watchers of Itral

The Watchers are well aware of the eye's effects on divination magic, while most who seek the eye do not know about these effects and cannot explain why normally reliable magics are so questionable. They use a variety of ritualized procedures to account for these disruptions, but for the most part these take time. Their innate ability to predict the near future during combat is unaffected, as they use mental calculations to deduce the most likely outcomes. Other procedures they use involve rituals that require 50 man-hours per level of the spell (or Challenge of the creature using a power, feature, or trait) to sort through the false readings as well as at least 10 castings of use of the divination magic in order to get a true reading. This has no effect on the divinations blackout that the eye generates within one mile of itself.

Eye Effects Table

1d6	Effect
1	You see a world beyond worlds, planets in orbit about strange moons, moons in orbit about massive creatures, the domains of gods, the vapors between matter, and the location of one person or object in your reality that you name. This final vision is as if you were a disembodied eye floating a few feet above them.
2	You see an image of the past from a random time and place in your reality. You can control the when and where of this vision with a successful DC 13 Intelligence check. The vision then changes to a panorama of strange beings dicing with planets for the fate of the universe, a twisted labyrinth of flesh and bone that screams as it tears itself into bloody pieces, and a vicious fight between three-headed dogs over the fate of a doomed soul.
3	You see a mighty ship sailing on a sea of mucus and blood, a library as large as the vastness of the open steppe but filled with books whose bindings are made from crawling shackled humanoids who moan and writhe against each other, the tiniest creature in all reality crawling upon an even tinier sphere of another reality, and eldritch insight into one skill granting you advantage on its next use.
4	You see a billion worms with the heads of humanoids crawling and writhing in a ball at the heart of a great glass globe as tentacled masses watch in amusement. A disembodied spinal column and brain cavort on a beach made of tears and bones, as waves of viscera wash up on shore. Two cats chase you across a field of razor-tipped grass blades. You gain proficiency in one skill you do not have proficiency in, but the knowledge fades after 24 hours.
5	The world becomes a tiny marble cast by gods into a sea of flaming mouths that speak the greatest truths of the universe in a chorus of babbling tongues. A dozen headless humanoids hold up a giant head that spews forth moons and stars as it tumbles like a beachball between their hands. The stars turn to skulls and pull themselves out of the tapestry of the sky, trailing strings of intestines as they cackle over your greatest failures and promise worse. Until the next sunset, you can cast a single 3rd-level divination spell once using Charisma as your spellcasting ability score.
6	Lightning crashes from a sky made of severed livers, as rain sweeps across mountains of rotting flesh as skeletons battle eternally beneath their peaks. A million chickens explode like a bursting star and fill the universe with feathers that form worlds undreamed of. A trout swims into your ear and lairs in your head and speaks the secrets to wealth and power at terrible costs. You have advantage on all attack rolls, saving throws, and ability checks until the next sunset, but then suffer disadvantage on the same until the following sunrise.
7	You see a great maw filled with teeth composed of thousands of goblins that swallows you. As you pass inside, you are in a whirlwind of arms and legs adrift on a sea of infinite mercury. Your greatest love and greatest enemy battle each other for your soul, and you do not recognize either. At the end of the visions, you become poisoned for one hour and gain a ravenous hunger for fried worm castings.
8	A face screaming your name pushes itself out of a kaleidoscope of colors that shift and flow like melted wax. A tavern filled with pigs dressed as people order platters of humans roasted in great ovens. Ostriches peck at a giant log within which hide all the people you have ever killed. You are unconscious for the next 24 hours and cannot be awakened by anything short of a *wish* spell.

| 9 | A mouth vomits out humanoids who plunge like a waterfall into a pool of slime that bubbles and churns. The world whirls around you and into you and through you until you do not know what is you and what is everything else. A hundred imps make sport with a hundred pixies as the gods look on and place wagers. Your Intelligence, Wisdom, and Charisma scores are reduced to 1 and return to their normal levels at the rate of 1 point per completed long rest. |
| 10+ | You see worlds spinning in a stew pot as a giant ladles each one out into a bowl and your friends feast upon the screaming millions. Eight elephants rear up and trumpet saliva in great spouts that wash the stars from the heavens and leave bats in their place. The sun drips red blood upon a hot plain of upturned faces frozen like sandstone. You are petrified and your soul is trapped within the eye until another person rolls this result and exchanges your soul into their body and their soul into the eye. |

To acquire the benefits of the *eye of Itral*, you must perform a lengthy ritual that costs 10,000 gp in rare spices, incense, and finely crafted ritual items. Once these components are assembled, you must perform an exacting eight-hour ritual from which you gain three levels of exhaustion. You can now attune to the eye.

Random Properties. The *eye of Itral* has the following random properties:
• 2 minor beneficial properties
• 2 major beneficial properties
• 1 major detrimental property

Increased Wisdom. After you are attuned to the *eye of Itral*, your Wisdom score increases by 2, to a maximum of 24. You can gain this benefit only once from the eye.

All-Seeing. The eye grants you truesight 120 feet. Furthermore, you have advantage on all Wisdom (Perception) checks.

Divination. You can stare into the eye without suffering any effects. After spending some time staring into the eye and receiving whatever visions it offers, you may choose to accept or ignore the effects.

Visions. You can use the eye to locate and view any creature on the same plane as you and up to three centuries into the past, as per the spell *clairvoyance* but you see and hear the target. You may cast spells through the magical sensor as if they were originating from the sensor.

Destroying the Eye of Itral. The eye must be covered in an even, five-foot-diameter sphere of alchemical salts taken from the Salt Skeleton. This salt sphere must then be encased in a sphere of mithral. Once this is complete, the alchemical salts must be ignited. After 24 hours, the outer casing of mithral can be cracked open to reveal a tiny marble-sized eye, which is rendered powerless.

FILTER MASK

This leather mask covers the mouth and nose. An inch-thick by three-inch-diameter oval case protrudes from the lower part of the mask, located roughly over the mouth, and can be closed with brass-hinged latches. An alchemical filter fits within the case and cleans the air as you breathe. The filters available in Cat's Cradle (found at any general store or shop specializing in mining gear) are a well-known protective device against the tainted air of the Salt Skeleton as well as "dead air" and other foul gases found in the salt mines. Each filter lasts for one hour, after which it provides little benefit. During this hour, while wearing the mask you automatically succeed on Constitution saving throws to avoid Salt Contamination. The filters do not protect against other airborne contaminants or gasses. A filter mask costs 25 gp, and weighs two pounds. Replacement filters cost 5 gp each and have negligible weight.

CULTIC DAGGER OF THE WATCHERS OF ITRAL

Weapon (dagger), uncommon

This curved dagger bears the eye symbol of the Watchers of Itral on its pommel. You gain a +1 to attack and damage rolls when using the *cultic dagger of the Watchers of Itral*. Furthermore, you may use the dagger to cast *augury* once as a ritual You may do so once and regain use of this ability following a one-hour ritual.

CULTIC SWORD OF THE WATCHERS OF ITRAL

Weapon (scimitar), rare

This scimitar bears the eye symbol of the Watchers of Itral on its pommel. You gain a +1 to attack and damage rolls when using the *cultic sword of the Watchers of Itral*. Furthermore, you may use the sword to cast *augury*, *clairvoyance*, and *legend lore* once each as rituals. You regain a used spell at each sunset.

www.ingramcontent.com/pod-product-compliance
Lightning Source LLC
Chambersburg PA
CBHW042108160726
48295CB00017B/1027